"Betsy, My Love..."

She lifted her face to look at him.

He kissed her then, his mouth soft and gentle on her own, and her lips met his, gave of themselves. Her body pressed against his; her every nerve leaped with pleasure. For a moment or two longer, she gave of herself in that kiss. Her body strained to his; she felt her senses leap and go mad....

Other Romances from SIGNET

- ☐ **OUTRAGEOUS FORTUNE** by Claudia Slack.
  (#W7894—$1.50)
- ☐ **FOR LOVE OR MONEY** by Vivian Donald.
  (#Y7756—$1.25)
- ☐ **SIGNET DOUBLE ROMANCE—LOVE ON LOCATION** by Vivian Donald and **THE HAPPY ISLE** by Vivian Donald.
  (#W7895—$1.50)
- ☐ **CAPTURE MY LOVE** by Mary Ann Taylor.
  (#W7755—$1.50)
- ☐ **GATEWAY TO LOVE** by Arlene Hale. (#W7803—$1.50)
- ☐ **IN LOVE'S OWN FASHION** by Arlene Hale.
  (#Y6846—$1.25)
- ☐ **LEGACY OF LOVE** by Arlene Hale. (#W7411—$1.50)
- ☐ **THE STORMY SEA OF LOVE** by Arlene Hale.
  (#W7938—$1.50)
- ☐ **A VOTE FOR LOVE** by Arlene Hale. (#Y7505—$1.25)
- ☐ **SIGNET DOUBLE ROMANCE—THE DAWN OF LOVE** by Teri Lester and **TANIA** by Teri Lester. (#E7804—$1.75)
- ☐ **SIGNET DOUBLE ROMANCE—DANGEROUS MASQUERADE** by Hermina Black and **A WORLD OF LOVE** by Hermina Black. (#E7703—$1.75)
- ☐ **ENCHANTED JOURNEY** by Kristen Michaels.
  (#Y7628—$1.25)
- ☐ **ENCHANTED TWILIGHT** by Kristen Michaels.
  (#Y7733—$1.25)
- ☐ **SONG OF THE HEART** by Kristen Michaels.
  (#W7702—$1.50)
- ☐ **TO BEGIN WITH LOVE** by Kristen Michaels.
  (#Y7732—$1.25)

THE NEW AMERICAN LIBRARY, INC.,
P.O. Box 999, Bergenfield, New Jersey 07621

Please send me the SIGNET BOOKS I have checked above. I am enclosing $_____(check or money order—no currency or C.O.D.'s). Please include the list price plus 35¢ a copy to cover handling and mailing costs. (Prices and numbers are subject to change without notice.)

Name_____

Address_____

City_____ State_____ Zip Code_____

Allow at least 4 weeks for delivery

My Treasure, My Love

by
Lynna Cooper

NAL BOOKS ARE ALSO AVAILABLE AT DISCOUNTS IN BULK
QUANTITY FOR INDUSTRIAL OR SALES-PROMOTIONAL USE.
FOR DETAILS, WRITE TO PREMIUM MARKETING DIVISION,
NEW AMERICAN LIBRARY, INC., 1301 AVENUE OF THE
AMERICAS, NEW YORK, NEW YORK 10019.

COPYRIGHT © 1978 BY LYNNA COOPER

All rights reserved.

 SIGNET TRADEMARK REG. U.S. PAT. OFF. AND FOREIGN COUNTRIES
REGISTERED TRADEMARK—MARCA REGISTRADA
HECHO EN CHICAGO, U.S.A.

SIGNET, SIGNET CLASSICS, MENTOR, PLUME AND MERIDIAN BOOKS
*are published by The New American Library, Inc.,
1301 Avenue of the Americas, New York, New York 10019*

FIRST SIGNET PRINTING, FEBRUARY, 1978

1 2 3 4 5 6 7 8 9

PRINTED IN THE UNITED STATES OF AMERICA

Chapter One

The big British Airways jetliner began its drop toward Heathrow Airport. Seated beside a window in that plane, Betsy Macon peered down at the terminal, telling herself she was being extremely foolhardy to waste her sabbatical leave by coming to England just to please a man she had never seen.

Still, the aura of mystery intrigued her.

Jason Tilden had hinted in his letter that she would stand to gain great wealth by humoring him. He had been a friend of her father, who had often spoken of him, telling of how in their youth, they had worked together on archaeological digs in the Near East, in Persia, and in India. Her father had told her of him, and of Rutherford Manners, and of how they had talked long and often, of how they had dug and sweated and labored over shards of pottery, of metal, seeking to uncover the riddles of the past.

Jason Tilden had never married, yet he had corresponded with his two friends, and Betsy had pleasant memories of her birthdays, when there would be a present for her from Uncle Jason. She had never met the man; her father had been away from his family at those times when he had been uncovering ancient artifacts; she knew only that the Englishman looked on her as a daughter and had followed her career at the university with great interest.

The plane dropped lower, lower.

Lynna Cooper

The ground was coming up to meet them; far away she could make out the long runway onto which the jetliner would soon be lowering, and then her visit to England would really begin.

Betsy sat back in the seat, her fingers making certain that the belt was secured about her middle. She knew that her heart was pounding in excitement; she wondered what wealth it was she stood to acquire—and what she might have to do to obtain it.

Jason Tilden was not a wealthy man; her father had assured her of this. Oh, he had enough to live comfortably, he owned a fine house at a place called Fosdyke near The Wash, but he had no millions to bestow. What, then, was this wealth of which he spoke? If he expected her to go gallivanting off somewhere to the far ends of the earth and dig around for buried gold—forget it.

She was no archaeologist, as her father had been. She taught English at a small university in the Midwestern United States. She was content with her life, she had no expectations of ever becoming rich.

Just the same. . . .

Betsy dreamed a little as the wheels of the plane hit the tarmac, as the engine roared in slowing down the big plane. She felt the drag, felt herself pressed back into the seat, and then the plane was slowing, the pressure was gone, and she felt a sudden exultation sweep through her.

She was in England. Her heart thumped excitedly; she glanced out the window at the activity of the airport; she touched her tongue to her lips.

It was early afternoon, it had been a night flight she had been on, and as she rose to gather up her handbag and coat, she told herself that there was a car waiting for her at the airport. She would have to be careful about driving in England, for she would have to drive on the left-hand side of the street, rather than on the right, as one drove in the United States. This was the result of long conditioning, she understood; in the very old days, when knights used to ride along the road, they went on the left so as to keep their swords free to draw. She smiled as she thought about that.

MY TREASURE, MY LOVE

She lost herself in the press of passengers leaving the plane; she went to the baggage counter to pick up her big valises. When a porter approached her, she surrendered the bags to him and followed as he brought her to the car rental counter, where she picked up her keys, then trailed him between the hurrying people, along a sloping ramp, and finally to a parking space where she saw a spanking new Hillman-Minx.

Within minutes she was moving away from the airport and out onto the big new highway, losing herself in the cars flowing away from Heathrow. She was very careful; she thought only of the car, of the traffic around her, telling herself that when she came to a corner, she must turn it, not as she did in the United States, but with regard to the laws of England.

She must head northward out of the London area; her first stop would be at Cambridge, where she would find a hotel and stay the night, then drive on to Fosdyke the next day. There was such a thing as jet lag, she recalled, owing to the time difference between the United States and England. She would retire early tonight and get plenty of rest.

She drove steadily through the day, pausing only at Stevenage for tea. With constant driving, she grew accustomed to the road and the car, and after a time she did not think about it.

Instead, her thought dwelt on what might lie ahead of her.

What was this treasure Jason Tilden had in mind? He had been cryptic in his letters, wheedling her by telling her the advantages of summering in England, of the enjoyment she would take in the countryside. And the treasure, of course. It was the treasure and her share of it that had decided her to forgo the trip to the Rockies which she had planned in favor of traveling to England.

She smiled at the thought of being a treasure hunter. It was so far removed from her rather humdrum life! She would happily welcome any adventure, she told herself. But what sort of treasure could it be, in England? There were no pirate hoards here, no wrecked ships with their holds laden with gold. Betsy told herself glumly that in all probability there was no treasure at all.

Lynna Cooper

Well, what difference would that make?

Jason Tilden had paid her travel fare; he would put her up in his house so that she would have no expenses on that score. Even if there were no treasure, she would have a far different holiday from those on which she usually went.

It was evening by the time she drove into Cambridge. She was scheduled to stay overnight at the Bull Hotel. Her eyes finally caught sight of its sign, and she levered the car toward a small parking space.

As she did so, a car horn blared at her.

Instantly her foot trod on the brake. Had she violated some English law, in some way of which she was ignorant?

"That's my space, lady," a voice called.

Betsy turned her head to see a glittering red sports car, the like of which she had never before seen. A man was leaning his head out the window, scowling at her.

"Your space? Did you pay for it or something?"

His tanned face lost its scowl, to be replaced by a glance of sheer annoyance. "Of course not. But I was occupying it until just now."

"Sorry," she caroled. "Finder's keepers."

She slid from the front seat, aware that her skirt was caught on the cushion and that she was exposing an extraordinary length of stockinged leg. To her annoyance, she saw that he was eyeing that leg in something like admiration.

Ignoring him, she went to the trunk and lifted out her overnight bag.

"Staying here?" he wondered.

"I am, for the night. Not that it's any business of yours."

She walked away, knowing his eyes were running over her. To her surprise, she did not feel indignation any longer. It had been a long time since a man had used his eyes on her in such a fashion. When she was at the hotel door, she turned and glanced back at him. He was still there, his head craned out of the window of that red car, staring after her.

Betsy tilted her nose at him and marched into the lobby.

A bath first, then a change of clothes. After that she would have her dinner in the big dining room. Then for a long sleep in her room. She hoped the bed would be comfortable.

She lazed in the bath for a long time, until she realized that the dining room might close if she dawdled much longer. She toweled off and slid into a green and white sunburst print by Leslie Fay. It had cap sleeves and a narrow belt.

Betsy surveyed herself in the mirror.

Her thick black hair was piled high on top and fell down about her shoulders, framing a suntanned face with big green eyes and long lashes. Her mouth was overlarge, but it seemed to fit into her face nicely enough. She was critical as her eyes swept over her features. Because that man had stared so long at her?

She shook herself. Certainly not! She just wanted to make certain that she was looking her best, was all.

Still! She had enjoyed his stare. It made her feel more like a woman.

Gathering up her handbag, she locked the door behind her and went down the elevator to the ground floor. As she moved toward the dining room, she saw that a man was blocking it, looking at her with cold eyes.

As she went to move past him, the man said, "Sorry, madam. The dining room is closed."

Betsy gaped at him. "Closed? It can't be! I'm starving."

"Sorry, madam."

Her nostrils caught the aroma of delicacies as she stood there, undecided. Oh, drat! Why had she lingered in that bath? Now she would have to go out and tramp the streets looking for a restaurant.

She was turning away when a male voice said, "Oh, there you are. Come in, come in."

She turned to see whom the man was addressing. A big blond man with laughing blue eyes was approaching the doorway, smiling at her. It was the same man who had been in the sleek red car earlier.

"It's all right," he was saying to the doorman, at the same time slipping a pound note into his hand. "She's with me, she's just a little late."

"Very good, sir."

The blond man reached out and hooked her arm with a

hand. "Come along, darling. I've told you again and again not to dawdle so."

Betsy opened her mouth to protest; but that hand on her arm was drawing her forward, and unless she wanted to make a scene, she was going to have to accompany him. She began to walk beside him, head lowered, seething inside, as his voice went on and on. She knew very well he was laughing at her, deep inside himself.

"You have to take the bull by the horns when you travel," he was saying, guiding her between the tables until they were at a table situated beside a big window. "Otherwise, you'll be pushed around all over the place."

He held the chair for her.

"Go on, sit down," he urged.

She sat. There was no sense in arguing with the man. Besides, she was hungry, and she had no intention of walking around Cambridge trying to find another restaurant. She saw a cocktail glass in front of his place. Apparently he was a late arrival himself.

"Thank you," she murmured primly. "I am hungry, you know."

He showed fine white teeth in a friendly smile. "Glad to hear it. I like girls with appetites. Now what will you have to drink?"

"Just some wine, please. Oh, and I'm paying for my meal."

She might as well get that in because she had no intention of being put under any obligation to this one. He was entirely too sure of himself.

He nodded, his gaze running over her dress. "I like it," he told her. "Its color sets off your eyes. They're like two emeralds, did you know that?"

"They're just green," she muttered.

"No, no. Don't ever think that. Those are emeralds, filled with fire and light. And you have the face and the hair to set them off."

Betsy stared at him. "You're an American, aren't you?"

He chuckled. "Does it show that much? Every Englishman I meet assures me that my voice gives me away." His eyes studied her. "But you're American, too?"

She nodded. "From the Middle West."

MY TREASURE, MY LOVE

"First name?"

"Betsy."

He held out that huge, tanned hand of his. "Hi, Betsy, I'm Jim."

She smiled and extended her own hand. It was caught and held firmly, and she sensed the strength in this man. His hand held hers for a little longer than was necessary, so that she had to apply pressure to pull it free.

"I'm having the curried lamb," he informed her. "I'd advise you to have the same. They have a good cook here, he worked in India for a time, and what he can't do with lamb and curry powder just can't be done."

He sat back and eyed her closely. "Are you on vacation?"

She nodded warily. She did not want to become embroiled with a perfect stranger here in England, American or no.

"I'm visiting a friend."

He nodded. "I am myself. I've just come from South America, where I was helping build a dam in Brazil."

"I'm a teacher," she murmured, deciding it was safe enough to tell him that.

"You don't look like a teacher."

"Oh? How do teachers look?"

His grin was friendly enough, and she decided that he meant nothing by his question. But something inside her bridled at it.

He waved a hand. "Every teacher I ever knew was either somewhat matronly or seemed half-starved. There are exceptions, of course. You're one of them."

"I think you're just making that up, trying to get on my good side."

He laughed. "Maybe I am. Most of the teachers I knew were men anyhow. Except for those long-gone days when I was in grammar school."

They sipped their drinks, talking about events of the day, the condition of traffic in England as contrasted with that in the United States. They both agreed that the roads in England were, once one was off the splendid highways, for the most part narrow and geared to times in which people traveled on foot, by horse, or in carriages.

Betsy found Jim friendly enough—though she did not

relish the way in which his eyes slid over her body from time to time—and he was quite content to chatter on, carrying the burden of the conversation. He was an interesting talker; he regaled her with anecdotes of his life as an engineer in the far corners of the world.

The lamb curry was perfect, she thought after she had swallowed a few mouthfuls. It was seasoned nicely, and there was plenty of it. The talk slowed to a definite stop while they ate and did not pick up until they were consuming berry tarts with coffee.

Then Jim asked, "Where away tomorrow? Or are you planning on staying here and seeing Cambridge and the countryside?"

"No. I have a—an appointment with a friend."

His blue eyes smiled at her. "Don't want to tell me where you'll be staying, do you? I may have some free time. I'd like to show you around."

"Oh? Do you know so much about England?"

"Worked here for a time. Got to know the place pretty well."

Betsy took a sip of coffee. She did not want to give this stranger her address; she did not want to tell anyone where she would be staying. Because of the treasure? N-no, not exactly, she thought. But if there was a treasure, she wanted to keep it a secret.

Talk of treasure sometimes brought out the worst in people.

"I'm just resting and relaxing," she assured him. "I plan on driving around and seeing the sights. Maybe I'll even go for a swim or two, if the warm weather keeps up."

"Where?" he asked.

When she looked at him, he grinned and said, "I merely asked you where you might be staying."

"I don't think I'd better tell you that."

His golden eyebrows lifted. "Not going to meet a lover, are you?"

Betsy laughed. "Hardly that, no."

"There's a mystery here of some sort. I can smell mysteries a mile away. Hmmmm. Not a lover. But it's something you don't want to talk about, obviously."

MY TREASURE, MY LOVE

She protested. "I don't want to be mysterious, but I would rather keep my destination to myself."

"Oh, of course. Whatever you say." He showed his teeth in a grin. "But if I run into you again, am I permitted to talk to you?"

"Don't be silly. Of course you can."

She wondered if he would trail her to Fosdyke in that red car of his. It would do him no good if he did. She was not going to take up with any casual man she might meet on her vacation.

They left the dining room with Jim holding her arm. Betsy was not sure that she liked this proprietary attitude of his, but she was not going to jerk her arm away. Let him hold it if he wanted. A fat lot of good it was going to do him.

Back in her room, she slid into a bikinied mini-sleeper and threw back the bedcovers. She paused then to turn and stare at her reflection. She was showing an awful lot of herself, she thought, then giggled. It was a good thing Jim wasn't here to see her in this bit of lace and polyester.

She fell asleep almost at once.

In the morning she ate breakfast by herself, vaguely regretting the fact that Jim was not here. He had been pleasant enough last night, friendly and talkative. If it hadn't been for him, she might not have been able to eat.

She was finishing her ham and eggs when he appeared and headed straight for her table. He was wearing slacks and a sports jacket, and his sports shirt was open at the throat. He looked very rugged, very sure of himself.

"May I?" he asked, pulling back a chair and not waiting for her consent.

His eyes ran over what was left of her ham and eggs, and he nodded. "Glad to see you eat a good breakfast. An important meal, breakfast. Too many women skimp on it."

"Oh? Are you an authority on women?"

He smiled. "Haven't had much chance to be, really. I travel over the world too much to settle down with any one girl. Not much sense in asking a girl to travel to Brazil or possibly to Saudi Arabia on the spur of the moment."

"Your work must be fascinating; you get to see so many foreign countries."

Lynna Cooper

He shrugged those wide shoulders almost casually. His eyes were going over her again, she noted. He was seeing the snugness of her sweater, which was strained somewhat across her chest, and she noted the approving look in his eyes. Really! She would have loved to be able to reach over and bop him one.

But she wouldn't be seeing him anymore, once they left the Bull. So let him look. Fat lot of good it would do him.

She even dawdled slightly over her breakfast, giving him time to order and eat with her. He was pleasant enough, she guessed. If only it weren't for those blue eyes that seemed to see so much of her all the time! And he didn't have any qualms about looking either. None at all.

He talked between bites of his food, telling her about Brazil, speaking of the Indians who frequented its jungles. From the Indians he switched over to tell of the nomadic Arabs who had come on their camels to watch quietly as he and his crew of men constructed a pipeline for oil. It came to Betsy that his life was as exciting and romantic as hers was dull and filled with routine.

He smoked two cigarettes and drank two cups of coffee before she began to push back from the table, lifting her grained leather tote bag and slipping its strap over a shoulder.

"It's been fun." She smiled. "But now I have to run."

His eyes got that amused look in them. "You sure we won't meet again?"

"Very sure. And now I really must be running."

He rose to his full height and walked beside her, saying, "I'll see you out. Somehow it doesn't strike me as right that a pretty girl like you should be wandering around unescorted."

"I'm quite able to take care of myself, thank you."

"I'm sure you are."

Was that laughter in his throat? She eyed him suspiciously, but he was only smiling down at her. Almost foolishly, she thought. Like the proverbial cat that had swallowed the canary.

She paid her bill while he stood off to one side. Then he was at her elbow again, walking her out to her car. He even took the keys from her and unlocked it, opening the

MY TREASURE, MY LOVE

door and standing to one side so she could slide in on the seat.

"Thank you," she murmured when she was inside, waiting for him to shut the door.

His blue eyes held hers.

Then, before she could move, he had leaned into the car and touched his lips to hers. Surprise held her motionless. She felt the weight of his mouth, and almost automatically her lips returned that faint pressure.

She pulled away, but it was too late.

He had felt her response.

"See you—I hope," he murmured, with laughter in his voice.

She opened her mouth to shout out her indignation, but he was slamming the car door and moving away. Her eyes glared at his broad back, at that athletic walk which carried him away from her so swiftly.

Her hand went to the door crank to lower the window, but it froze there. What could she possibly say? Say? Yell, rather, because he was a good distance away by this time.

"Oooooh," she breathed. "Oooooh!"

She backed out and drove away, not glancing in his direction. She was only about fifty miles from Fosdyke, she would be there by early afternoon—travel in England wasn't as fast as it was in the States—and then she could relax and forget all about Jim—

Jim what? She did not know his name, just as he did not know hers. Oh, well. It didn't matter.

She drove through a flat countryside, seeing occasional farms dotting the landscape, with cows and a few horses cropping the grass. It was rural and pleasant and reminded her a little of Illinois. In the distance she could see a church spire rising against a blue sky dotted with white clouds.

She crossed the River Ouse and drove toward Ely. The sun went behind some clouds, and there was a brief rain shower. Wiper blades swinging back and forth, she drove more carefully now, listening to the drumming of the drops on the car top. But soon enough the rain was gone, the sun was out again, and it was as if there had never been a shower.

Lynna Cooper

She was moving now through a section of the countryside that was called the Isle of Ely on her map, even through there was no island, just a continuation of the flat landscape. The signposts showed her the names of towns, and she read them off with laughter gurgling in her throat.

Wisbech Saint Mary, Parson Drove, Cowbit, and—some distance away—a place known as King's Lynn. Betsy thought to herself that she must find a book, somewhere, which would tell her the origins of such names. It would be fascinating reading.

She was thinking about lunch even as she approached Whaplode Drove and was trying to decide about whether to have a salad or a sandwich when a car horn began honking. Glancing up into the rearview mirror, she saw a red car come roaring along, and without seeing the driver, she knew who it was.

It came up on her with a rush and was past almost before she could blink. An arm was thrust out the window, waved. Then the car was gone around the next bend in the road.

Betsy sighed. At least, he wouldn't be around to have lunch with her. Or kiss her again! He was in something of a hurry to get where he was going, it seemed. She wondered where he was headed in such a hurry.

She ate lunch in a pleasant little tearoom in Spalding, half expecting at every mouthful to see Jim walk into the place and stride toward her table. Betsy admitted she felt vaguely disappointed when he did not appear.

Fosdyke was not so far now. Only about ten miles away. She should be there well within the hour, she decided as she folded her road map and tucked it back into her bag. She lingered over a cigarette and her coffee, wondering what Jason Tilden would bè like.

Her father had spoken of him often enough, over the years. He was a brilliant scholar, a born archaeologist. He had written papers for many of the most prestigious publications; he had lectured at Cambridge, at Oxford. Betsy wrinkled her nose. He was probably dry-as-dust, somewhat peppery, and even obnoxious.

And what was his purpose in bringing her over here?

MY TREASURE, MY LOVE

Why let her share in any treasure he might find? She was a complete stranger to him, and outside of a snapshot or two of her that her father may have mailed him in the past, he had never laid eyes on her.

Oh, well. It was fun being here anyhow. If she could not get along with him, she could always pack her bags and take a car trip around England. As long as her traveler's checks held out anyhow.

She drove on from Spalding, relaxed and comfortable. To her right now she could see Whaplode Fen and, farther on, the flat extent of Holbeach Marsh. Salt marsh and peat fen lay everywhere. Yet it was pleasant land; she could see fields of corn growing and flowers lifting their heads into the sunlight along the edges of the road.

When she came to Fosdyke, she pulled over to the side of the road and opened her tote bag. Fumbling about, she drew out the letter Jason Tilden had written her, giving her directions on how to find his home. She read them over, glanced at the road ahead, then nodded.

Within fifteen minutes she was swinging the Hillman onto a narrow road that brought her between trees to a big house. Betsy let her eyes run over it as she slowed.

It was certainly imposing!

A low fence of stone ran all around it, and inside the fencework, green grass lay like a carpet everywhere. The house itself was also of stone, with a great number of chimneys rising from the slate roof. The windows were narrow, for the most part, though on the first floor there were wider ones, all with leaded glass. A vast door was of oak, reached by a number of stone steps.

"Middle sixteenth century," she murmured, and felt excitement rising in her.

It would be fun to examine such a house. There must be hundreds of little rooms and cubbyholes in that place. Imagine one man living there alone. It did not seem right, somehow. There should be a huge family with a lot of children running up and down stairs, with laughter and the sounds of conversation echoing everywhere.

She drove slowly toward the front door, turned off the motor, and climbed out.

There was no sign of life. Could she be mistaken? But

no, she had followed the instructions in that letter exactly. This had to be the place.

Betsy marched toward the door.

She put out her hand toward the bellpull just as the door opened.

A man with a small beard, neatly clipped, stood smiling at her. He was no taller than she and seemed lean and hard. He wore a woolen jacket, a sweater under it, and slacks of some Scottish clan's plaid. He was beaming at her, and in his sharp black eyes there was quick appraisal.

"You're even prettier than your pictures," he said, holding out his hand. "Come in, Betsy, come in."

She felt her hand squeezed; then he was moving to one side, gesturing her to enter. She stepped into a huge hall, the walls of which were hung with antlers, so many of them that she stared unbelievingly. Below them were clustered ancient shields and swords, pikes and gisarmes.

"I love it," she whispered.

His chuckle was soft, contented. "This place is my pride and joy; it's home and wife and mother to me. I've kept it much as it was years ago, when it was built and lived in by Michael de Blesherham.

"Who was Michael de Blesherham, you ask? He was a knight who served King Henry the Eighth. He was banished from court because he fell in love with a pretty girl on whom the King had cast his eyes."

Jason Tilden shrugged. "Michael and his pretty girl eloped and were married, and they came here to build this home for themselves. It's a pretty story, and fortunately it has a happy ending.

"They had a large family, many sons and daughters. That family lived in this house for more than three hundred years. Only in the last century did they die out, and the house was put up for sale. It has had a number of owners since then, but none of them cared for the old place.

"I was fortunate enough to buy it many years ago, when land values around here were not what they are now. It's always been a haven for me. Even on my field trips to far places, there was the reassuring knowledge that this was here to welcome me when my task was done.

"But come, you must see the rest of it."

MY TREASURE, MY LOVE

He hesitated then. "Ah, I forget my duties as host. It's been so long since anyone has visited me. Would you care for some lunch? No? Then some tea, certainly, and a biscuit or two."

His hand touched her elbow, guiding her forward under a great archway into a big room filled with heavy furniture, with thick rugs on the floor and a vast fireplace in which, Betsy thought, an entire deer might be roasted. There was a settee before the hearth, with end tables on each side.

"Make yourself comfortable, my dear. May I call you Betsy?"

She laughed. "But of course. We're going to be good friends, I hope."

"The best. Already I look on you as the daughter I never had."

Betsy smiled. "I should have thought a man like you would have wanted a son, rather than a daughter."

"Oh, I have a son. You'll meet him in a moment."

He turned and walked away, leaving Betsy staring after him in perplexity. Her father had told her Jason Tilden had never married. He was the only one of the three friends who had never found time to take a wife. Yet now he claimed to have a son? It made no sense.

Unless, of course, his son had been born out of wedlock.

Betsy moved toward the fireplace, staring at the coat of arms, somewhat worn and eroded now, which was set into the stonework above the mantlepiece. In those old times this must have been a busy room, with a huge log flaming away during the fall and winter and early spring. In the cold weather they must have burned a lot of such logs.

She turned, lifting off her tote bag and putting it on a table.

Then she froze, staring at the man who stood in the archway, grinning at her.

"I knew it," he exclaimed. "I just had a feeling."

Jim walked toward her, his face breaking into a grin.

Chapter Two

Betsy backed up a little, staring in disbelief.

"What are you doing here? Did you follow me?"

He came to a stop, looking injured. "Follow you? Of course not. I've been here some time. It's just that I figured, back there in Cambridge, that a lone American girl on her way north just had to be Betsy Jane Macon."

"You're Jim Manners."

"I am." He laughed. "I guess I'm the son old Jason was referring to when he was speaking to you. You see, I've known old Jason for some time. When I was in England working from time to time, I stopped by to make his acquaintance. We became good friends."

Betsy scowled at him. "Then you know all about this treasure?"

"Well, no. Old Jason has been mighty secretive about that. Oh, I knew a long time ago that he had hidden gold on the brain. But he didn't trust anyone, or so it seemed. Or maybe it was because his researches weren't complete."

"What researches?"

Jim Manners spread his big hands. "Well, now. If you were to discover some sort of treasure, would you want to spread the word around indiscriminately? You'd keep it to yourself until you were certain of it. Wouldn't you now?"

"I suppose I would, yes."

"Well, then?"

Betsy scowled. "Are you trying to say that Jason Tilden

has found his treasure or knows where to look for it? And that he's asked us here to share it with him?"

"Exactly."

"I don't believe it."

He stared at her. An irritated expression touched his tanned features but faded soon enough as he ran his eyes over her. Then he smiled and shook his head.

"You're the most cautious girl. Why else do you suppose he sent you the money for your plane fare and invited you here for the summer?"

"But it doesn't make sense! Look, I know he mentioned a treasure to me, and it's been in the back of my head ever since I received his letter. Sure, sure. I want just as much as anyone to get my hands on a treasure. But why should he? Will you tell me that? Why should he share any of it with us, always assuming he knows where there is a treasure?"

"May I answer that?" asked a voice.

Jason Tilden stood there with the tray in his hands. On it were cups and saucers, a big pot of steaming tea, and a platter filled with biscuits. Betsy exclaimed and ran toward him.

"Here, let me take that. You'll drop it all."

Jason Tilden beamed at her. "You're just like the daughter I never had, Betsy, how I imagined she might be if I'd been lucky enough to have one. Just as Jim here is the spitting image of what I've imagined a son should be."

She carried the tray to a table and set it down. Her cheeks were flushed, from pleasure at his compliment or annoyance at the thought that she had played the fool by coming here, she wasn't sure.

Her hands poured the tea, handed out the cups, then took her own cup and retreated to a big wing chair, where she sat and began to sip the tea. It was delicious, hot and fragrant, and as she swallowed, it seemed almost to calm her. She sat back in the chair and eyed both men.

"Well? Let's have it," she murmured.

Jason Tilden beamed at her, nodding his head. "You Americans. Always you dig right to the heart of the matter. Well, why not?"

He frowned thoughtfully, and Betsy understood that he

MY TREASURE, MY LOVE

was trying to find the proper words for what he had to tell them. She sipped at the tea, aware that Jim was running his eyes over her again, in that way he had. She darted him an angry look, but he only winked at her.

The older man asked slowly, "What do you know about King John, Betsy?"

She stared. "You mean Richard's brother? Richard of the Lion-heart—that is, the Crusader?"

When Jason nodded, she went on. "Well, when Richard went off to the Crusades—the Third Crusade, that is—he left John here to run the kingdom for him. John liked being king; he wasn't at all happy when Richard finally came back to the throne.

"His turn came when Richard was killed by that crossbow bolt while he was besieging the castle of Châlus. And so John, his brother, came to the throne. Now John was nicknamed Lackland, for he had no property to speak of in his name, though, of course, his father—that was Henry the Second—gave him the earldom of Cornwall and later the lordship of Ireland."

Jason Tilden rose and moved toward a table on which was a rack of pipes and a big tin of tobacco. He filled a pipe, but before he struck a match to it, he swung about and smiled at Betsy.

"I'm asking you about all this ancient history to make sure you know the background of the treasure," he said slowly, and then struck the match.

When his pipe was drawing nicely, he nodded slowly and began to speak again.

"John was a misfit. By blood he was a Plantagenet, but he was a coward, he was vain and haughty, and I think myself, he didn't have a brain in his head. Still, they made him king of England, overlooking Arthur of Brittany's claim to the throne.

"John made a poor king. He made mistake after mistake. He had Arthur murdered and divorced his first wife to marry another woman. He was cruel and treacherous, not at all a nice man."

Jason sighed. "He quarreled with Pope Innocent, and when he lost his argument, he began stealing from the church. He waged war unsuccessfully; he angered and out-

19

Lynna Cooper

raged his barons. The end result of all this was that they forced John to sign the Magna Carta, as I'm sure you know.

"Well, it seemed that John would never learn. Even after signing the Magna Carta, he had his troubles, troubles which he brought on himself. His barons rose up against him, and John took the field against them. In October of the year 1216, John was at King's Lynn with his followers, and with his royal treasure."

Betsy sat forward on the edge of her chair, heart pounding, mouth a little open. In his quiet way, without inflection or any other signs of excitement, in that dry-as-dust voice, he nevertheless managed to hold her enthralled.

"His barons were hot on his trail. They wanted to overtake him, capture him and the royal treasury, and perhaps execute him or depose him. At any rate, King John left King's Lynn—which is on the southern coast of The Wash—and fled northward to Swineshead on its northern coast. Behind him came the baggage train that held the treasure."

Jason Tilden smiled at Betsy; his black eyes grew fond. It was as if she really were his daughter, she thought. And that was silly. But she liked this little man, his intensity, his obvious eagerness to please.

"That treasure never arrived at Swineshead. Whether or not the baggage train took a different route from King John isn't known, though it's been suspected by historical scholars that it did. At any rate, it cut across the low waters of The Wash . . . and disappeared.

"There are quicksands in that part of The Wash—or were, in those days. Since then, of course, a lot of that land has been filled in. Where the baggage train disappeared is now at least fifteen feet below the surface of the ground."

Jim Manners stirred restlessly.

"That shouldn't be too much of a problem, always assuming we know their route of march."

Jason Tilden nodded slowly. "Yes, and I've made a study of that. I've examined all the old manuscripts, I've even obtained a letter—a copy of it to be truthful—written by one of the men who was with the baggage train.

20

MY TREASURE, MY LOVE

It was found in an old castle some years back, and a friend of mine let me make a copy of it.

"I think I can tell you almost exactly where the baggage train perished. I've walked over the ground and studied it. All we need do is to put down a drill, and I'm certain we'll locate it."

He leaned back in his chair and beamed at Betsy, then at Jim.

Betsy licked her lips. She was dubious about all this. Of course, she understood that no treasure in the world lay on top of the ground for the picking up. There was always work involved. At the same time. . . .

"Why?" she asked. "Why are you willing to share it with us?"

Jason Tilden turned his pipe over and over in his fingers as he frowned down at it. Twice he began to speak, then stopped. Finally, he looked right at her.

"I've never had any children. Always I have looked on you two as my own, or almost so. And I have had a dream." His smile was tender. "I've dreamed that you two children of mine would marry and—"

"Marry!"

The word burst out of Betsy.

She straightened and looked hard at Jim Manners. His face was bland; there was no surprise on it, no hint of shock, such as she was feeling. Could it be that he knew about this harebrained idea of Jason Tilden's? She wouldn't put it past him.

Jason looked distressed. He sat up and fussed with his pipe, looking at Betsy in bewilderment.

"Why, yes. I've thought about it; I've kept in touch with you both. I know neither of you is romantically attached, that neither has been married. Is the idea so distressing, my dear?"

"It's out of the question. Absolutely," she snapped.

Jim Manners uncoiled his big body from the chair in which he was perched. He came to his feet, and his blue eyes smiled down at her. Betsy scowled at him.

"It's just a business proposition," he said softly.

"It's crazy."

21

"Not so crazy. We get married, we share in this treasure. Right, Jason?"

"Correct. Once you two are married, we can begin work." Jason was speaking crisply, almost anxiously, as his eyes rested on her. "It's a whim of mine, this marriage, it's the answer to a long-held dream.

"Your fathers were—and are—the best friends I ever had. Oh, I've thought about your marriage ever since you were born. Jimmy here first, by three years, and then you, Betsy. Just right, I used to tell myself. All I had to do was bring you together, and I felt you would fall in love."

"Forget it," Betsy muttered.

Jason sighed, but Jim Manners only smiled.

"Why not let Betsy and me talk this over, Jason? We can go for a spin in my car and talk."

"Fine. Go ahead, you two. Take a ride. But be back in time for dinner."

Betsy rose to her feet. It was on the tip of her tongue to tell them both that the only ride she wanted to take was in the Hillman, to leave this place and never come back. But she was tired; she supposed it was the jet lag that all jet-plane passengers got when they traveled into different time zones.

She wanted to crawl into a bed and sleep. She didn't want to drive off somewhere and try to find a hotel or a rooming house.

"All right," she found herself muttering. "I'll go for a ride, and I'll talk. But I want you to know that I have no intention of getting married. None at all."

Jason Tilden was disturbed. He shook his head; he frowned and seemed about to speak. There was misery in his eyes, and Betsy guessed that the old man had thought about their marriage for so long he just couldn't believe anyone would oppose it.

Betsy felt sorry for him suddenly. She moved toward him, caught his hand in both of hers, and squeezed it. Her heart went out to him; she could picture his years of loneliness and how he must have dreamed of these two "children" of his, how he had pictured their marriage with him standing by and beaming his blessing at them.

"I'm sorry," she whispered.

MY TREASURE, MY LOVE

He nodded, his eyes averted. Were there tears in those old black eyes?

Betsy shook herself. If she weren't careful, she would be letting her emotions get the better of her. Marriage was out of the question. That was final. Definite. There was nothing to be said on the subject which would change her mind.

"Let's go," Jim murmured, taking her elbow.

She let him lead her from the room, but when they were in the hall and out of sight of the older man, she jerked her arm free and turned to stare up at him.

"Get this straight," she snapped. "I'm going for a ride, but I have no intention of letting myself get conned into marriage."

"What have you against marriage?"

"Nothing. Someday I hope to fall in love and be married. But certainly I don't intend to marry just to please an old man's whim."

"Neither do I."

She gasped. "You don't? But—"

He smiled down at her. "Will you come along?"

His hand caught her arm and propelled her along the hall and out the front door. They walked along a slate pathway that took them to the back of the big house.

When Betsy saw the maroon car, she stared.

"What is it?" she wondered.

"A Shelby Cobra GT 500-KR."

She looked up at him. "I've never even heard of it."

His shrug was casual. "Probably not. There aren't too many of them around. It's an extravagance of mine, I'll admit. But I have to spend my money on some luxuries."

"Do you have so much money?"

He opened the door and watched her slide in on the seat. He said, "Enough. It's hard to spend money in the wilds of Brazil or Saudi Arabia. I bank what I earn, and I earn good money."

He closed the door and moved around to the driver's side. Betsy ran her eyes over the dashboard and studied the plush interior, comparing it to the Hillman she had been driving. She wondered how much money he had spent, to buy a car like this. Her eyes slid sideways at him.

23

Lynna Cooper

He was handsome enough, she guessed. Big and rugged, the outdoors type. But something bothered her. If he was so prosperous as to be able to afford a car such as this, what need had he for any buried treasure?

"Why?" she asked suddenly as the car moved along the narrow, winding country road. "Why are you so interested in finding that treasure? If it can be found, that is. You seem to be doing all right."

"I'm between jobs." He grinned. "Got to go back to the States in September, where I'm to build a dam, down in New Mexico. Figured it would be fun to look for lost gold."

His eyes turned toward her briefly. "Doesn't the idea excite you?"

"Well, of course it does. It isn't every girl who gets a chance to go hunting for treasure."

"Then what's the problem?"

She stared at him disbelievingly. "Are you serious?"

He chuckled. "Is the idea of marrying me so distasteful?"

"It isn't just you."

"That's something, at any rate. I thought maybe you felt I had some sort of infectious disease."

"Oh, don't be silly."

They drove along the road until he made a turn that brought them, in time, to a little hill that looked out over the calm waters of The Wash. It was a peaceful scene, with the sun setting and a small sailboat moving lazily across the water.

"Now then, let's talk," he suggested.

"You can talk all you want. I'm not marrying you."

"Hey, it needn't be for life."

"For me it does."

His blue eyes regarded her carefully. "Are you one of these romantics? I didn't believe they existed anymore."

"They do. At least, I do." She turned to face him more fully. "When I marry, I want it to be for love. I want to spend the rest of my life with my husband, caring for him, sharing his life. I don't want a marriage where I'm just a— a *reason*."

His eyebrows lifted. "A reason?"

"You want to dig for that treasure. The only way you

MY TREASURE, MY LOVE

can do that, I guess, considering what Jason Tilden told us, is to marry me. Therefore, you're willing to marry me. Phooey on that."

He chuckled. "I get it. You want me to romance you, bring you flowers, take you out on dates." His face became thoughtful. "You know, that would be a switch, wouldn't it? I marry you; then I romance you. How does that sound?"

"As crazy as Jason Tilden's idea."

"No, think about it. You don't have any special boyfriend, do you?"

"Certainly not."

"Then why not? We get married, I'll romance you, and maybe you'll even fall in love with me."

"No way."

There was a little silence. Then he asked almost plaintively, "Am I so hard to take?"

Betsy smiled. "You're a very good-looking man, Jim. You have a fine job, at least I assume you do, and I think you'd be a fine catch for any girl."

"Well, well. We're making progress. So I'd be a fine catch for any girl, would I? Then why not for you?"

"Oh, can't you understand? I don't love you; you don't love me. What chance would our marriage have?"

"As good a chance as any. No, don't huff and puff. Just listen. You must know guys and girls who've gotten married all starry-eyed and wishful. Then, in a year or less, they're fighting like cats and dogs, they're talking about getting lawyers, and in a few months they begin divorce proceedings."

She knew several couples like that. It was one of the reasons why she shied away from marriage. So she was old-fashioned. So she wanted to marry a man and love him dearly all their lives. What was so wrong about it?

When she admitted knowing such people, he nodded seriously. "Ours will be a little different, that's all. The marriage ceremony comes first, then the romancing."

Laughter bubbled from her lips. "And in the meantime, while all this romancing is going on, you'll be having your fun with me."

His blond eyebrows rose. "Oh, so that's it, is it?"

25

"What?"

He leaned closer to her, and she caught the smell of tobacco and some shaving lotion. "You don't want me to bed you if I marry you."

"I do not. Not, that is, until—"

"Until what?"

Betsy kicked at the floor mat, realizing she was talking herself into a corner. All her life she had longed for and expected a romance, at some time or other. So far she had not even caught the faintest sniff of one. Until now, of course. And this wasn't a romance; it was just a cold-blooded business deal.

"Until we fall in love," she almost whispered.

Anger flooded up inside her. She faced him, eyes brilliant. "Is that so surprising? Are you so cynical in your approach to love and marriage that you can't understand what I'm saying?"

"Hey, relax. We're friends, remember. Or I think we are." He grinned at her. "We aren't married, so we can't be enemies."

"I didn't say that."

"You intimated it."

His big hand reached out suddenly and caught hold of hers. He squeezed, not hard but gently, as though he were trying to tell her something. Tears came into her eyes, and her lips trembled. She hated herself when she got like this, all weepy and dissolving inside herself. But she meant what she had said. She did!

She didn't want a cold-blooded marriage; she wanted love and romance, kisses and hugs and—other things. But not because of any treasure! No amount of money could take the place of love. Maybe she was silly, maybe she was schoolgirlish, but she didn't care. That was the way she was.

When she sought to free her hands, his grip tightened.

"Let me hold them. Please?"

She glanced at him and was surprised to see the affection in his gaze. He nodded at her look.

"You make me remember myself when I was young. I used to daydream a lot in those days, telling myself that somewhere in this world of ours there was a woman for

MY TREASURE, MY LOVE

me. A girl, rather. We would be the happiest couple in the world. We would go off and laze away the days on a hilltop, with the clouds moving overhead, and turn and kiss every so often."

She slid her eyes sideways at him. Was he feeding her a lot of nonsense, something he imagined she wanted to hear? But no. His face was dreamy; he was not looking at her but staring off down the slope toward The Wash.

He felt her eyes on him, turned, and smiled faintly. "I lost those ideas as I grew older, but I rather imagine I'll keep some of those notions as long as I live. They're a part of me."

"I'm surprised you could abandon them so easily."

He seemed startled. "I didn't know I had."

"We-ell, here you get an offer of a treasure if you marry me, and you're all for it."

"Maybe there's something about you I like."

Betsy sniffed. "You don't know anything about me."

"I know enough."

"I could be a scold. A—a harridan."

"Not you."

There was an assurance in his voice that surprised her. He was still gripping her hands; he was holding them as if to guard them, as though telling her that she was safe with him. It was a good feeling, Betsy felt. For too long a time she had been dependent on herself alone.

What was she thinking about? In a few more minutes of this, she would be telling him he could marry her!

She sought to free her hands again, but he was too strong.

"Give it a try," he murmured.

"Give what a try?" she asked, though she knew the answer.

"Marrying me. No, don't shout out yet. Let me talk." He drew a deep breath. "Go through the marriage ceremony. Listen, will you? Just listen! We'll get married, but we won't act like married folks. We'll sleep in separate beds; I won't lay so much as a finger on you—unless you want me to, of course.

"Will you hold still?"

She faced him, cheeks flushed, eyes bright, well aware of

27

that big hand which imprisoned both of hers. Somehow or other he had come closer to her so that his body was touching hers. She was practically leaning against him, and the touch of his body was somehow reassuring.

"It's ridiculous," she snapped.

"Why? Maybe it's fate. Maybe Cupid chose this way to bring us together. Sure, I could be wrong, but there's the possibility, isn't there?"

Well, it *could* happen that way, she supposed. It went against all the rules, but maybe there were no hard-and-fast rules when it came to finding somebody you could love and live with. She thought of her mother and of how she used to tell her that she considered her father a fly-by-night, traveling all over the world to earn a living as an archaeologist.

Her father and mother had met at a country fair. They had danced together; they had eaten sugar candy side by side, laughing and talking. For three days her father had called on her and taken her out to eat, to ride around the countryside. Then he had left for the Near East.

He had written to her from time to time, and when he had come back, he had asked her to marry him. Her mother had had misgivings, but she had said yes. She had even accompanied him on some of his digs after that. Only when she herself had been born had her mother remained in the States while her father went off to wherever his occupation called him.

They had made a go of marriage. Of course, in time her father had taken a post at a university, where he taught archaeology. But in the beginning. . . .

"But it seems so—so silly," Betsy protested. "I mean the mere idea of our getting married just to please an old man is utterly absurd."

"Oh, I don't know. You'd be pleasing me, you know."

Betsy grew aware that their eyes had been almost locked together for the past few minutes. They had been staring at each other as though each sought to read in those eyes some indication that what they were contemplating doing was not beyond the bounds of common sense.

His hand squeezed both of hers. "Why not give it a try?"

MY TREASURE, MY LOVE

She shifted uncomfortably. "The whole thing is so ridiculous!"

"But it is romantic?"

Betsy laughed. "Yes, I'll give you that."

"Then why not? Look, you can always divorce me if—given a little time—you decide that marriage with me is not for you. I promise not to touch you or hug you or kiss you unless you invite me to do so."

"You really mean that?"

"Honest Injun. Cross my heart."

"We-ell. . . ."

His big hand again squeezed both of hers. "Good girl. Now we're engaged. Here, let me. . . ."

He reached into his jacket pocket, brought out a small box. He opened it and lifted out a ring that contained a huge diamond. Betsy stared at it, her heart beginning to hammer.

"How come you had that with you?" she asked suspiciously.

"Just on the off chance I might meet a lovely girl and—"

"No. Tell me the truth, Jim."

He looked embarrassed. "All right. I've known for a long time that old Jason had his heart set on marrying us two. When I used to visit him, he talked about it off and on. I also knew you were coming over here, and I knew he wanted us to get married."

She stared at him, not quite believing him. "Do you mean to tell me you bought that—that *rock!* just on the off chance I might marry you? You didn't know what I looked like or—"

"Well, now, I had a sort of idea about that."

"But how?" she asked bewilderedly.

"Your father and Jason used to write each other a lot. Your father sent him photos of you over the years. Last one I saw was taken a year or two ago, as I recall."

"Now what picture would that be?"

His eyes lighted up, and Betsy squirmed uncomfortably at what she read in them. Deep inside her a sudden suspicion leaped to life, and she opened her lips to exclaim.

"Not the one in—"

"The bikini. Right."

29

He laughed. "I stole it from Jason, or maybe he let me take it, I'm not sure. But I've carried it with me ever since."

She remembered the occasion very well. She had been in a somewhat daring mood at the time, she had gone off with the family to that lake in Wisconsin for a holiday, and she had bought a white bikini. It had been a somewhat daring thing, it showed entirely too much of her body; but she had been with her family, and when she wore it, she got a lovely tan—almost all over.

Dad had taken a picture of her in the bikini. At the time it had been a great joke; she had struck a sexy pose, and he had snapped the shutter. She had forgotten all about it until now.

"Do you have it with you?" she asked innocently.
"Carry it everywhere, in a special part of my wallet."
"I've never seen it."

He eyed her suspiciously. "You want to see it now? Okay."

Jim reached into his hip pocket, brought out his grained leather wallet, and then extracted a small glossy snapshot. He held it in his hand so that she could see it.

Betsy bit her lip as she felt the flush rise up into her face. It was even worse than she had thought. That picture showed her long, slender legs, her bare midriff, the fullness of her breasts. True, the white bikini showed off her long black hair, which framed her face, but the hair was not nearly so long as she would have liked.

She made a grab for it, but Jim held it away, laughing softly. And as she struggled to take it, her action brought her up against him, body to body. Too late she realized that she might be tempting him.

She started to draw back, but his right arm went around her and held her.

Then he kissed her.

His lips were firm, and she sensed the hunger in them. She struggled, but his right arm was too strong. He kissed her gently at first, then more strongly.

She really fought him then, ashamed of the fact that her lips had betrayed her. She had actually kissed him back! And she had enjoyed it. Oh, yes! Something deep inside

MY TREASURE, MY LOVE

her had responded to him, to his maleness, to those lips of his.

Breaking free, she panted. "You said there were to be no hugs and kisses between us!"

"That's after we're married or until you give me some sign that you want me to kiss you."

"You're disgusting."

"No. I think I've fallen very much in love with you. It's only natural to want to hug and kiss the one you love."

"Love," she sneered.

He slid the snapshot back into his wallet. Despite her anger, Betsy noted that he did it almost reverently and with a faint smile on his mouth. She eyed that mouth, noting how strong it was, how shapely. She wished her heart would stop its slamming; it seemed to be telling her that she was enjoying every moment of this, and of course, that was a big fat lie.

"Now we'll go tell Jason that we're going to be man and wife," he murmured.

Betsy scowled. That had better be some good treasure! If it wasn't, she was just making an utter fool of herself.

Chapter Three

The marriage took place in the little church in Fosdyke.
Betsy wore the traditional white; she had shopped in one of the stores early in the morning, had found a white summer dress that fitted her perfectly, and had bought white shoes to go with it and even a tiny veil. She knew the white dress set off her tanned face and thick black hair; she knew, too, that Jim Manners had stood stock-still when he saw her in it, his blue eyes wide and filled with admiration.

Hah! Let him stare if he wanted. A fat lot of good it was going to do him! Still, Betsy admitted to herself that she liked his staring; it showed that he thought he was getting a beautiful bride.

Jason, too, was ecstatic. He came over to her to clasp her hands, gazing at her with tender eyes.

"You're more beautiful than I had thought, Betsy. You're actually radiant. But then they say that all brides look so on their wedding day."

"This is just a business proposition with me," she murmured.

He shook his white head, smiling slightly. They were out of earshot of Jim Manners at the moment, so he leaned closer and whispered, "You may think so, my dear, but these wise old eyes of mine look below the surface."

Now what had he meant by that? Surely, he wasn't trying to imply that she loved Jim Manners or could ever do so? If he was, he was mistaken. She was doing this only to get her hands on that hidden gold or a good share of it.

And that was an odd thing, now that she thought about it. She had never in her life been mercenary. Always she had been something of an idealist.

No matter! She had agreed; she would go through with it.

In the little church she made the proper responses, as did Jim. Jason Tilden was the best man, and for the maid of honor there was a neighbor of old Jason, a woman in her thirties named Honor Furlong, who was beside herself with excitement.

The ceremony did not last long. It seemed to Betsy that she spoke and acted as in a dream, and when Jim slid the golden wedding band upon her finger, she stared down at it as though not knowing what it was. When he released her hand, she touched that wedding ring as though it might vanish off her finger.

Then they were walking out into the morning sunlight, and Jason was telling them that he had arranged for a bridal luncheon at a nearby restaurant that overlooked The Wash. Jim took her arm, guiding her toward the Shelby Cobra, with Jason Tilden and Honor Furlong following.

"Isn't this exciting?" Honor was bubbling, walking behind them. "A childhood romance, imagine."

Betsy glanced at Jim. "A childhood romance? What sort of story have you been making up?"

"I couldn't tell the truth, could I? The treasure must remain a secret. Until we actually find it anyhow."

Betsy subsided but gave him a sharp look. Childhood romance indeed! Just wait until she had him off to herself. She'd tell him about childhood romances!

The restaurant where Jason Tilden took them was a very pleasant place. Long ago it had been a big boat shed, but it had been refurbished and set with windows which looked out over the waters of The Wash. The interior was hung with old fishing nets, with harpoons and buoys cluttering the walls; its tables were draped with cloths festooned with pictures of whales and dolphins.

Jason brought them to a nook, waited until they were

MY TREASURE, MY LOVE

seated, and then beamed around at them. "I'm going to propose a toast," he explained, "just as soon as the drinks arrive."

And when those drinks had come, he lifted his glass of Scotch and murmured, "To this moment, which is the fulfillment of a lifelong dream."

Honor bubbled, "Jason, you must tell me more. Were these two really childhood sweethearts?"

"They were indeed. They first met on a farm in Wisconsin, where they were staying with their families. They liked each other from the very first, and on the day that Jim saved Betsy from a bull—well! You can imagine."

Betsy was aware that her mouth was open. She closed it firmly, glancing at Jim, who looked so modest that she could have kicked him.

"A bull?" she asked weakly.

"You remember the monster, darling. It was big and black, and it had a white spot on its head. It went for you with its head down, and those horns were the longest and sharpest I've ever seen."

Honor Furlong exclaimed, "My goodness! You must have been terrified."

Before she could shake her head in denial of any of this fairy tale, Jim was saying, "Well, of course she was. She just stood there, unable to move. Fortunately I ran toward that bull, yelling and waving my arms. It saw me and veered away, so that I could run to her and grab her arm.

"She woke up then and we raced for the fence together. Bet was always a good runner. She never ran faster than she did that day, though."

Betsy shook her head wonderingly. Was she crazy, or were they?

"And since then? Have you two been keeping up a correspondence or anything like that?"

"A few letters now and then," Jim admitted. "But over the years we did drift apart, I'm afraid. I had to earn a living, and since I studied engineering, my jobs took me to all corners of the world."

"And now you met here," Honor bubbled. "That's all your doing, Jason, I take it."

"Well, I've known Jim a long time. He's been in England

Lynna Cooper

before. And when he told me about his childhood sweetheart, I realized I could play the fairy godfather. Since I had known both their fathers when I was in the digs in the Near East, I wrote to Betsy and invited her here to spend the summer with me."

His impish face was very pleased.

"She knew nothing about Jim coming here, naturally. That was my surprise. But when they saw each other, they almost fell into each other's arms."

"It's amazing," Honor murmured. "Just amazing."

It's a lot of hogwash, Betsy told herself. But she would not spoil the day by saying anything. She would just sit here like a good girl and let those two make up all those lies. At least, she thought morosely, it's probably better than the truth.

The dinner was a great success. The drinks loosened them up, and the roast beef with Yorkshire pudding was really something else. Betsy discovered that she was ravenous, and the others ate with just as much gusto as she, though Honor kept murmuring that she would gain weight if she ate like this every day.

For dessert there was chocolate mousse, with coffee.

Then they were moving out toward the car, and Betsy found herself wondering about sleeping arrangements. There was no way she was going to slide into the same bed with Jim Manners, husband or no. This was a business arrangement, pure and simple. She took his arm as they walked toward the car—only as a blind to throw Honor Furlong off the truth—and when he opened the car door for her, she gave him a big smile.

When he got a pleased look on his face, she murmured, "Honor's watching us."

His face fell, and Betsy exulted.

They drove Honor to her house, a pleasant little cottage about a half mile from Jason's big stone house. Honor hugged and kissed her and wished her all the happiness the world had to offer.

Then they were on their way home.

Jason sat in the back seat, but he was seated on the edge, so that he could peer between them, at their faces. He was very excited, whether because of the marriage or

MY TREASURE, MY LOVE

because now he could reveal what he knew about the treasure, Betsy was not sure.

"The happiest day of my life," he kept muttering, "The happiest. You two don't know how long I've looked forward to this. It's as if my every dream has come true."

"And mine," Jim said, nodding.

Betsy wanted to kick him.

When they entered the house, Jason caught both their arms and brought them with him into his den. The room, lined with bookcases from floor to ceiling, held a desk and chair and a big easy chair that had a reading lamp behind it. This was where Jason spent the days when it rained and his evenings.

He ushered Betsy to the big leather easy chair and indicated that Jim was to sit behind the desk. He himself stood before them, smiling at one and then the other.

"Tomorrow," he said, "we go to work. The treasure is there, I know it. All we have to do is locate it, then dig it up."

Jim frowned. "Hold on now, Jason. Other men have sought that lost treasure of King John. I've read about their attempts. What makes you so sure you know where it can be found?"

"A map. A map that was drawn by Ranald de Cressy, who was one of the royal secretaries and who traveled with King John to Swineshead, where John died within the week. Or if this Ranald did not draw it himself, it was drawn under his supervision.

"For Ranald was faithful to John, one of his constant companions who was always with him. For a long time the map was lost. Forgotten. Indeed, I doubt whether any man knew it existed."

Betsy could not help the excitement that flowed in her. Inch by inch she moved forward on her chair, eyes wide and excitement churning inside her.

"How did you find it?" she wondered.

Jason Tilden turned and smiled at her. "By a very odd circumstance, my dear. For years, a very good friend of mine named Henry Travers collected old manuscripts. He was left a lot of money by his father, and he put this money into the purchase of rare old books and manuscripts. From time to time we would write to each other.

"Henry was a recluse of a sort. He traveled a lot, always by himself, and he advertised that he would pay top money for any books and maps and manuscripts which were offered to him. It was always a condition of his purchase, of course, that he be allowed to look at whatever was offered before he made his decision.

"Well, it seems they were tearing down an old building which had been part of a fourteenth century castle. They broke through a wall and found in a small room a few old chests, half-rotted and eaten by worms. Somebody thought of Henry Travers and got word to him.

"Henry bought the chests and all they contained at a good price. Oh, he'll make a fine profit on his purchase, but that's neither here nor there. This map was hidden away in one of those chests."

Jason Tilden brooded, sitting on the edge of his desk. "As I've said, Henry Travers was my friend. He wrote me that he had an old map, very stained and dirty, but one that obviously showed The Wash and part of its surrounding countryside. He wondered if I might be interested in it.

"Well, of course, I was. I went to visit him, and when he showed me the map, I recognized the signature of Ranald de Cressy. Now I'm no historian, but I've read a lot, and I knew that Ranald was one of King John's friends. So I bought the map and brought it home with me.

"Here, take a look."

He crossed the room and knelt at the base of one of the bookcases, where a series of low, flat drawers were built in. One drawer he opened and lifted out a length of dry, crinkled sheepskin. On its surface, Betsy could see half-erased words and lines.

Jason Tilden carried the map to his desk and spread it out. Betsy rose and leaned on the desk, scanning the map with puzzled eyes. She could make nothing of it. Oh, there were wavy lines and those half-erased words, but it seemed utterly useless to her.

When she said so, Jason chuckled.

MY TREASURE, MY LOVE

"Oh course, it's useless, as it is."

Jim Manners regarded him thoughtfully. "Now what do you mean by that?"

"One would have to know the topography of the land to understand this map. Whoever drew it knew that topography. In those days—back in 1216, when it was drawn—this map was as exact a copy of this area as could be had.

"I studied this thing for close to a year before it finally dawned on me. The map is precise *for its time*. It could scarcely take into account the changes that have come upon that land it pictures in the intervening seven hundred and sixty one years, now could it?

"So I drew two maps myself. One I made from this one, the other from the best modern map I could find. Let me show them to you."

He went to that same narrow drawer and lifted out two lengths of oilskin paper. He brought them back to the desk and spread them out. One was a duplicate map of the sheepskin map, only clearer in its detail; the other was obviously a copy of a modern one.

Jason Tilden laid the oilskin papers on top of each other. He spent a little time lining them up, but when he was done, Betsy could see for herself the changes in the shoreline that had taken place since 1216.

"It's incredible," she murmured.

"But true. The land over which King John rode, the dirt and pebbles that his horse's hooves kicked up are fifteen feet down from the present surface. Much of this area had been filled in, you know. A lot of the marshlands around here have been reclaimed. When King John rode over that land, it had none of its look at the present time.

"From what Ranald de Cressy wrote, I could trace King John's route of travel from King's Lynn north to Swineshead. As accurately as possible, that is. Somewhere along that route, as I've mentioned, he lost his wagon train that contained his treasures."

Jason Tilden sighed. He moved across the room to remove one of his pipes from the rack, and after crossing to a table where his humidor rested, he removed the top and began filling the pipe bowl. Betsy watched him, frowning slightly.

Was it really possible to know where King John rode those many centuries ago? More important, could one trace the passage of his wagon train? She supposed there had been a lot of treasures in those wagons. After all, King John would not leave so much as a farthing behind him for his enemies to seize.

"What sort of treasure was there?" she asked.

The older man turned from the humidor to smile at her almost wistfully. "Such treasure as a man may dream on, my dear. There was a royal crown, for instance, the golden crown of Germany which John's grandmother, the Empress Matilda, carried out of that country when she came to England. And—this is something I would give my eyeteeth to find— Tristram's sword."

Betsy stared. "Tristram's sword? You mean the Tristram who was from Cornwall, who was one of Arthur's knights?"

"The very one. And there is a tiny piece missing from the sword, that part of it which was buried in Morholt's brainpan when Tristram slew him." Jason Tilden paused to draw flame into the tobacco, puffing out smoke. It wreathed his head for a moment so that he seemed to speak out of a cloud.

"Poor Tristram. One of the strongest of the knights, who fell in love with a woman who was married to his cousin, King Mark of Cornwall. And because of her, he died."

There was a silence, during which Betsy thought about the ship that was bearing Yseult to Tristram and about the mistake which caused a black sail to be hoisted instead of a white. Watching for that sail, seeing the black, and losing hope, Tristram had died.

"What else was in the treasure?" Jim asked.

"Gold and silver cups, all of them fitted with rare jewels, rings, goblets, golden crosses, and rubies and emeralds almost beyond the counting. Together with a great hoard of gold coins. It was the royal treasury, remember.

"Its value today is fantastic. Just for its historical in-

MY TREASURE, MY LOVE

terest, it's worth millions of pounds. And can you imagine the worth of those golden coins, the way the price of gold itself has risen?"

Enthusiasm made Jason move up and down the room, waving his pipe, from which smoke rose up, like a baton.

"I tell you, it's the greatest treasure in the world. Matched only, perhaps, by the lost treasure of Attila the Hun, which is supposed to be at the bottom of the Danube River in Hungary. Men say the Huns altered the course of the river so as to hide Attila's burial place. I don't know about that. But nobody's changed the site of King John's treasure. It's still there where it was back in the year 1216. Waiting to be claimed. Waiting—for us."

He stopped before the maps, tapped at them with the stem of his pipe.

"These show us his route of travel. We know from historical accounts that he crossed The Wash just about where the Willestrem River meets the Glen, right at the beginning of The Wash. Now there are strong tidal flows right at that point. The fresh water from the rivers runs down to meet the incoming tide, and where they meet— right about at the spot that King John had chosen to cross—there is a lot of turbulence."

Jason made motions with his pipe.

"I myself think King John made a blunder. He should have waited until the tides subsided. But then I imagine he wasn't sure how close behind him the pursuing barons might be. And he wanted to cross over and reach that monastery at Swineshead. Perhaps he made an error of calculation. No man can know exactly. All we do know is that he chose to cross, and his wagon train with him. Or behind him, to be precise."

There was a little silence. Betsy found herself thinking about that moment when the tidal flows met and surged together, when the wagon train was caught by them and swept under those swirling, foaming waters. She seemed almost to hear the shrill screams of the men and horses as the waters inundated them, sweeping them sideways. She could see in her mind's eye the wagons tilting and going over, the horses trapped in the traces, kicking and flailing and entangling themselves all the more. Nothing could save them. They were beyond human help.

Ah, and King John! What thoughts must have passed through his head at that time? Before his eyes he could see the wealth of all England being swept away. Everything he needed, all he counted on were lost to him. No wonder the man had ridden like a madman to Swineshead and there had eaten and drunk until he died!

She sighed and glanced at Jim. He was studying the maps, a thoughtful look on his face. His finger tapped the top map.

"There were quicksands here, you said?" he asked.

"Yes. The wagons went down in them. And there they are to this day. Waiting to be raised up, waiting to be given to the world."

"This will require quite an engineering operation," Jim said slowly. "I doubt if the three of us can do it."

"Once we locate the wagons, we can hire men to do the digging. With our modern apparatus it should not be too difficult a task."

"What about equipment?"

"I've made the arrangements. We'll have a drill and a donkey engine at the spot I've picked. We can begin work tomorrow. Or the next day."

Jim glanced at Betsy. She saw the amusement in his eyes and stiffened. "I know how to work," she muttered.

"It won't be easy," he said gently.

"It will be worth a little sweat, if we can do it." Her eyes challenged him. "Can we? Can we do it?"

He shrugged. "We can try."

Jason Tilden had been watching them closely, his eyes moving from one to the other as he puffed on his pipe.

"Others have tried, and failed. It's only fair to tell you this." He put the meerschaum down and studied them both. "Every ten or twenty years the bug bites somebody, and he has a go at it. So far everyone has failed, though I will admit some things have been brought up by the drills. Bits of gold and suchlike things, threads from cloth and bits of rotted wood have come from the wagons no doubt.

"But it's down there, all right. All we need is patience and perhaps a good bit of luck."

MY TREASURE, MY LOVE

Jim reached for the maps, began to roll them up. "We'll start tomorrow," he told them. "But for now we all need a good night's sleep. We've had enough excitement for one day."

Jason snapped his fingers.

"Of course. It's your wedding night. I'm sorry. I've been so excited about this treasure I forgot all about that."

Betsy had not forgotten. She gave Jim a dark look, which he did not see. If he thought he was going to play the part of loving bridegroom, he might as well forget it. It was no loving bride he was going to sleep with tonight. As a matter of fact, he was going to sleep by himself.

Panic touched her for a moment.

Where *was* he going to sleep?

Not with her certainly. Not even in the same room if she could help it. Still, they had to act a part for the sake of old Jason. He must not suspect that their marriage was simply one of convenience. Convenience? It wasn't even that. She had married only because she was hopeful that they might find the treasure. Once they had done that, she would take her share and say good-bye to them all.

She rose now, hands clinging to her handbag. "I'd better get upstairs and get undressed," she muttered.

Jason Tilden chuckled. "You have an eager bride, my boy. I'm happy for you."

Jim himself looked dubious, though. And well he might, Betsy told herself. He was not going to find any eager bride, that was for sure.

She murmured a farewell and marched out into the hall. She ran up the staircase, heart thumping. Why had she allowed herself to be put in such a spot? Greed. That was the answer. Plain and simple greed. Well, no matter. Not even if Jim dumped the whole treasure at her feet would she consent to share a bed with him.

She ran into the bedroom and closed the door.

For a moment she waited in the darkness before turning on the light, telling her heart to stop its wild beating. She had no husband—no real husband, that is. This was not her wedding night. Well, what the world meant by a wedding night anyhow.

Legally, she was married. She could scarcely deny that.

43

But there was a world of difference between the legality and the fact. She just hoped Jim Manners would understand that.

Her hand switched on the light. The first thing she saw was the big double bed where she had slept last night. It was a roomy bed, plenty large enough for two people. Betsy scowled and looked around the room.

There was no other place for her husband to sleep but that bed.

Her lips tightened. Too bad.

She moved toward the dresser and reached behind her to run down her zipper. She stepped out of the dress and lifted it, staring at her reflection. She had chosen white underthings, and against that whiteness the flesh tints of her body stood out. She turned and eyed herself in profile. She had a fine body, she had always taken good care of it, and she supposed that it would appeal to a man.

No matter!

What was she thinking of, dawdling like this and entertaining such thoughts, when Jim might walk in on her at any moment? She turned to eye the door. A mere turn of the knob would permit him to enter.

She had better hurry.

She was lifting a leg to step into her pajama trousers when she heard his feet moving along the hall. She hurried so much to get that leg in proper place that she came close to losing her balance.

"Wait," she yelled. "Wait!"

She slid in one leg and then the other, then reached for the pajama top. She got into the jacket and was starting to button it when the door opened. Muttering under her breath, she managed to finish with the buttons.

"You're beautiful," Jim whispered from close behind her.

She swung about to find him standing about three feet away. His eyes went over her slowly, in that irritating manner of his, and she felt herself flushing.

"Couldn't you wait until I was in bed?" she snapped.

"What? And miss such a vision?"

Betsy snorted and turned away, moving toward the bed, knowing that those blue eyes were eating at her. She tried

MY TREASURE, MY LOVE

to be casual about the whole thing, she bent to throw back the covers and then slid under them.

"Leave a little room for me," he said.

She sat bolt upright, clutching the bedclothes to her. "You certainly aren't going to sleep in here with me! I hope you understand that!"

"But you're my wife."

Was he laughing at her? Betsy frowned, staring at him. He *was* laughing. Inside himself, of course. There was merriment in his blue eyes, though his face remained grave.

"That's just a formality, and you know it."

He came closer and sat down on the edge of the bed.

"You're beautiful, Betsy," he whispered. "I don't believe you realize how lovely you are."

"Flattery will get you nothing."

"I only make the remark to indicate that I am a grateful husband."

"Grateful?"

Suspicion was alive in her. She knew this man was only pleading his case, that he hoped by sweet words to charm her into permitting him to share her bed and her body. Well, there was no chance of that. She would sleep alone, and so would he.

"Of course, grateful. Suppose you'd been cross-eyed and all blotchy? Brrr."

"What difference would that make?"

His eyes opened wide. "I hope you don't think I married you just because we might find a treasure?"

Betsy stared. When she realized her mouth was open a little, she shut it. "That's exactly why you married me," she stated firmly.

Jim Manners shook his head. "Oh, no. No way."

She studied him for a long moment. Was he just telling her this to ease her off guard? Why else would he make up such a monstrous lie? She wished he would look away from her with those direct blue eyes. They seemed to reach down inside her and touch something deep within her that responded to them.

Angrily she kicked out with a foot under the covers. He was the most annoying man! Imagine hinting that he had

45

not married her for the treasure! Why else had he done so then?

"Do you?" he asked gently.

"Do I what?"

"Want to know why I married you?"

"No."

Hmmmm. That was not exactly the truth. She did want to know, very much. Out of the corners of her eyes, she looked at him. He was staring down at—

Hurriedly she lifted the covers the better to cover herself. Just like a man. An animal, really. "Stop staring at me," she hissed.

"Can't help it. I'm like the little boy who's had his face pressed to a sweets shop window for weeks on end, admiring the big chocolate bunny, and then finds he has it, right in his hands."

"I'm no chocolate bunny."

He smiled. "Indeed you're not, and I'm grateful. Once one eats a candy like that, it's all gone. But you now, you'll always be with me."

"I will not. Once we find that treasure, I'm leaving."

Jim Manners shook his head. "No. I'll never let you go."

She sank back into the pillow, her eyes locked with his. "You're the strangest man. What good can I possibly do you?"

"You're the fulfillment of a dream."

"You're crazy."

He rose to his feet and began unbuttoning his shirt. Then he pulled it out of his slacks. All the time he kept on staring down at her, at her thick black hair spread out on the pillow, at her body where the covers outlined it.

When he undid his belt, she asked weakly, "You aren't going to get undressed in front of me, are you?"

"If you don't want to watch, close your eyes."

She caught the laughter in his voice and turned over in bed, giving him her back. Oh, let him take his clothes off, if it made him feel male and superior. It would do him no good. He was not—repeat, *not*—going to get into this bed with her. She would sleep on the floor if need be.

The bed sank as he sat on its edge. Sighing, Betsy turned

MY TREASURE, MY LOVE

to glance up at him. Fortunately he was wearing pajamas. Rather loud ones, too, in alternating stripes of purple and gold.

"Now what?" she murmured.

"Don't you want to know why I really married you?"

"Okay, okay. Tell me."

"Because I fell in love with you long ago."

Betsy turned more fully so that she could stare at him. "That's impossible! You never saw me before the other day."

"I saw your picture, remember?"

"You mean that snapshot?"

"I've carried it with me for more than two years now. Every once in a while I'd take it out and stare at it, and I'd tell myself that one day the girl in that picture was going to be Mrs. James Manners."

"I don't believe it," she muttered.

"Still, it's true. Now how about a good-night kiss?"

"Oh, go away."

"I will, once I get that kiss. I have a sleeping bag I intend to dive into just as soon as you kiss me good-night."

"I won't."

The bedcovers were lifting as he swung himself about so that he could slide in under the blankets with her. Betsy swung about and, forgetting that all she wore were rather thin pajamas, began to push him away.

"Kiss?" he asked, capturing her wrists with his big hands.

He was staring down at her body again, and there was no way for her to cover herself. Flushing, she tried to pull her wrists away, but he only smiled and shook his head.

"Kiss first. Then I'll go sleep by myself."

"I'll never—"

She felt his leg thrust in under the covers.

"All right, all right," she yelped.

His lips were on hers then, and they were soft, yet bold, hungry, and demanding. Betsy felt her flesh react to that caress; her body seemed almost to lift up by itself to respond to it. One of his arms was about her shoulders, half-lifting her, hugging her.

Her senses swam. She ought never to have married this man. She should have known it would end like this, with

Lynna Cooper

his forcing himself on her. Against her will she responded to that kiss; she gave him her mouth.

And then he was gone, standing beside the bed and nodding down at her.

"I was right. I knew it," he said softly, almost to himself.

She could not speak; her heart was thundering away, and her mouth was a little open as she stared up at him. What was the matter with her? A mere kiss had never affected her this way.

"Wha-what do you mean?" she blurted.

He winked at her, touched his hand to his mouth, and blew her a kiss. "Go to sleep, my darling. I'll see you in the morning."

He moved to the wall switch, and the room was dark. She heard him fumbling about and sensed that he was sliding into that sleeping bag of which he had spoken.

Angrily she turned on her side and stared into the blackness.

She would have to watch him and his kisses from now on. They affected her in some strange way she did not like to think about. Yes, she would have to be very careful where this husband of hers was concerned.

Chapter Four

Betsy woke to morning grayness and lay a moment, snug and warm under the covers. Her eyelids flickered, then opened wide. Had that been a dream, all those things that she remembered? A wedding, and then last night, Jim Manners sitting on the edge of her bed and kissing her?

She lifted her head, peering. She could not see him, and so she threw back the covers and crept across the top of the bed.

He was sleeping soundly—or seemed to be—covered over by that sleeping bag. Betsy scowled, staring down at him. His blond hair was all tousled from sleep, and he looked much younger than he was, lying there. He was much like an overgrown boy, she thought.

Boy? Ha! It had been no boy who had kissed her last night, holding her so tightly she could scarcely breathe. Betsy frowned. She would have to watch those good-night kisses. This man had a way with him.

Her eyes ran around the room. Dared she leave the bed and change into her clothes, here in full view of him? She glanced back at this husband of hers, saw that his eyes were closed and that he seemed to be sleeping peacefully. Betsy scrambled out of bed, moved to the bureau in which she had placed her clothes, drew out a clean set of underwear, a pullover and a pair of slacks.

She unbuttoned her pajama jacket standing before the mirror. In it she could see the sleeping bag and his face. She was about to shrug off the jacket when it seemed that his eyelids fluttered. Holding the jacket about her, she whirled to stare.

His eyes were closed.

Still, he might have lifted them and then, when he saw she had seen him, lowered them again.

"I'll dress down the hall in the bathroom," she muttered.

"Spoilsport."

It was a whisper, no more. Yet Betsy glared and snapped, "So you are awake. I thought as much."

His eyelids lifted fully now, and he grinned at her, that confident grin which she had come to despise. Deep inside her a voice whispered, "You wanted him to look, Betsy Jane. You did, you did!"

She snorted her denial of this voice, snatched up her garments, and moved toward the door. "I'll dress in the bathroom down the hall."

"I can't get over it, a nice girl like you being so shy with your husband. Seems to me you'd want your husband to watch you getting dressed. It would certainly show a husbandly interest."

"You're not my husband," she said coldly. "If I had a real husband, one I loved. . . ."

"Go on," he said with a smile. "Don't stop now."

Betsy sniffed and moved toward the door. She'd better not give him any ideas because she had a vague suspicion that all this man would need might be a hint that she wasn't as cool to him as she appeared. If she weren't careful, if she gave him so much as a hope that she would respond to his advances, she was certain that he would leap out of that bag and tumble her on the bed.

She opened the door but paused to look back at him. His eyes were roving over those thin pajamas, and despite the fact that she held her garments before her like a curtain, she felt that he could see just about all of her.

"If I had a real husband," she told him, "a man I loved, that is, there isn't anything I wouldn't want him to do."

He threw off the sleeping bag, and Betsy ran.

Cheeks flushed, she took refuge within the bathroom, making certain the lock worked. Well! You were almost begging him to grab and kiss you again, Betsy Jane! Have you no shame?

MY TREASURE, MY LOVE

"Pooh! I can handle him," she murmured.

But she wasn't really all that positive, she admitted. True, she might be able to handle Jim Manners, but what about herself? If this body of hers was going to betray her, what was she going to do?

"I'll have to be careful. Very careful."

When she was dressed, she walked down the hall to the bedroom and hesitated with her hand on the knob. Was he dressed? How would he act when she entered? No matter. She was in control of herself now.

He was clad in slacks and a T-shirt when she went in. He turned from the mirror where he had been rubbing a hand over his jaw as though to test the toughness of his beard. He smiled at her, and Betsy was struck with his gentle strength.

"You're beautiful," he murmured.

"You need a shave," she told him.

"You're right, of course. I was just standing here thinking about our morning kiss and—"

"*What* morning kiss?"

His blue eyes went wide. "Why, the kiss to match our good-night kiss, of course. Don't tell me you're one of these wives who never kiss their husbands in the morning?"

"I do not."

She brushed past him to hang up her pajamas, very much aware of his big body and its controlled strength. If he turns around now and grabs me, I'll die. I just won't be able to fight him off!

He did not, though. He moved toward the door and went out into the hall, carrying his kit. Betsy sneered. A real man would have grabbed her and kissed her, even fought her a little if she had tried to prevent him.

She sighed. What's the matter with me? I want him to kiss me, but if he had done so, I would have been furious. Betsy shook her head. She was a sensible girl, always had been. It was just all these unusual things that had happened to her lately, that was all. She was upset, and she had every right to be.

She sat on the edge of the bed, waiting. It might not appear proper for her to go down to breakfast ahead of

51

him. After all, Jason Tilden assumed they were really man and wife. No need to let him know.

When he came back, he paused in the doorway, smiling happily. "You waited. Good girl. Now we can eat together."

"I didn't want old Jason getting funny ideas," she muttered.

He nodded. "It's best he doesn't. Until we see about that treasure."

It occurred to Betsy that she had forgotten all about the treasure, but she said nothing about that. Let him think what he would. She rose and moved toward the door, and he followed.

Jason was in the kitchen, scrambling eggs and frying ham. He turned to beam at them. "How are our two lovebirds this fine morning?

"Happy as two larks," Betsy found herself saying.

Jason's beam grew sunnier. "I'm glad. It makes me happy that I've brought you two together. Now sit down and I'll have breakfast ready in a moment. There's fresh orange juice, just squeezed."

They ate with the two men talking about the treasure, while Betsy eyed this brand-new husband of hers surreptitiously, avoiding his eyes but managing to take in his every feature. There was strength in his face, humor at his mouth, and she could see the bulges of muscle on his arms and shoulders. He seemed relaxed, completely at his ease.

His wife wasn't all that easy, she told herself grimly. All Jim Manners was concerned with was a treasure. She herself didn't give a fig about the treasure right now. She had acquired herself a husband, and she didn't know how to handle him.

Oh, she'd done all right so far. But in the days—and especially the nights—that lay ahead, she wasn't at all sure that she could keep up this attitude of hers. Jim had a way with him, like a big, friendly dog. You couldn't really get mad at him. Ha! And before you knew it, you were petting and fondling him.

She smiled to herself at the notion of petting and fondling big Jim Manners. He was more likely to be the

MY TREASURE, MY LOVE

one to do all the petting and fondling. She scowled. There was no way he was going to do that. Not to her at least.

"What about it?" Jim asked.

Betsy came out of her reverie. "What about what?"

"You're coming with us, aren't you? Jason has everything ready. We're about to do a little drilling this morning."

"Oh, sure. I'm coming along."

"Good girl."

His eyes lingered on her body for a moment, then lifted to stare into her eyes. Betsy stiffened at what she read in those blue eyes. They told her clear as clean glass that he wanted her. Oh, my. Yes. Hurriedly she bent and finished up what remained of her ham and eggs.

Her hand trembled slightly as she reached for the coffee.

She had to get control of herself. Jim Manners was man of the world enough to read the signs she was giving him. He would know that with a slight nudge or something like it, she would fall into his arms. She had to be on her guard.

He reached out for her hand, and old Jason smiled. She let him hold her hand and squeeze it. Why not? They were only playing a game for this older man, who had brought them together.

"Ready, darling?" he asked.

"I'm ready," she muttered.

They drove from the big stone house down the graveled drive and out onto the main road in the Shelby Cobra, with Jason in the back seat. Betsy listened to the powerful throb of the motor and noted how easily Jim handled the car. He would be like that in all things, she felt. Once he put his hand to something it would respond to his touch.

Ah, but would she?

That thought troubled her as they drove along the road with the salt marshes ahead of them and the peat fens off to one side. This was lonely country here; one could see a good many miles in a glance, for it was all flat country. The road itself wound and twisted here and there, and she told herself that this was the way it had been many centuries ago, when these present roads were mere lanes used by the farmers and peat cutters over the years.

Fields of corn lay around them, and in the distance she could glimpse more than one church spire. It was a peaceful land, with the sun shining brightly overhead and with a faint sea breeze stirring the corn tassels. Betsy sat back in the seat, very relaxed, her eyes drifting out across the fens.

"Years back nobody ever lived here," Jason was saying. "It was an out-of-the-way place, and in the very early years of our history, when men used rivers as roads, traveling on them in boats or beside them on foot, no one at all lived in the fens.

"In those days there used to be forests around here, but the fens killed many of those trees, some of which grew to almost incredible proportions. I've read of one felled tree that was ten feet in diameter. Can you imagine such gigantic trees? A massive sinkage of the land caused the peat bogs to form, burying many of those trees."

Betsy listened, enthralled. This land about her was so different from the country in which she had been born and reared.

"These fens are very widespread, aren't they?" she asked.

"They are, though at one time they covered far more territory, almost half of what is now Lincolnshire. In modern times the fens have been covered over with landfill to some degree, though here you can see them as they were long ago. The Coritani, a British tribe, lived in these parts. They fought the Romans from their hill forts; they were overcome and brought their tribute of corn along Ermine Street, which the Romans constructed as far as Lincoln."

Jim slowed the car and made a turn onto a dirt road at Jason's suggestion. They drove for about two miles, and then Betsy saw the donkey engine and the drill housing, standing in the sunlight.

When the car stopped, Betsy got out and wandered toward the engine, studying it with eyes that saw it only as a piece of machinery. She supposed that if they were successful in their venture, this engine would be very

MY TREASURE, MY LOVE

important to her, but right now she was more interested in the glint of sunlight on The Wash and on the Welland River where it meandered between its banks. Seeing a grassy knoll a dozen feet away, she moved toward it and seated herself.

Behind her, Jim and old Jason were working on the engine. In a moment she could hear the throb of its motor, a strange sound disturbing the placidity of the day. She turned and watched them for a little while, saw them fitting the drill into position.

After a time she rose and began to walk along the riverbank. She wandered aimlessly, without purpose, glad of this chance to exercise her legs. When she returned, she saw that the drill was hard at work; she heard the rhythmic sound of the donkey engine; she watched Jim move here and there, checking all the fittings.

This was not an area that was favorable to people. It was sparse, swept eternally by winds and sea breezes. She could imagine the peat cutters at work, lifting out the squares of peat which were used for fires by the people who lived in these parts.

She walked toward the donkey engine.

"Anything I can do?" she offered.

Jim smiled at her, a mechanical reaction, she felt. He was so intent on what he was doing that she understood he had forgotten her presence. He gave her a shake of his head and turned back to his task. Betsy walked away, striding along at a regular pace.

She was moving over the peat bog that intruded here almost to the edge of the river when she saw the man. He was running bent over, as though he wanted to escape detection.

He was not a big man; he was clad in a loose sweater and dirty trousers; he was unshaved and half bald. He soon threw himself flat on the ground and became invisible. Betsy stared across at the spot where he was lying, wondering who he was and why he was here.

Obviously he was spying on Jim and Jason. He had found a portion of ground that was slightly raised, which gave him a good view, yet he was hidden well enough.

When and if Jim lifted his head to look around him, he would certainly not see the man.

Betsy debated. Should she alert them that they had a visitor who seemed very much interested in what they were doing? She doubted that the man had seen her. He had been looking ahead of him, and she was slightly off to one side.

Casually, so as not to alert the watcher, she strolled back toward the throbbing donkey engine. She saw the drill emerging, saw Jim moving to lift it upward, out of the soil.

"Jim," she called. "Jim, someone's watching."

He turned toward her as she walked toward him, and she knew now that she had captured his attention. He moved to shut off the engine and stood there waiting until she came up to him.

"Did I understand you correctly? Someone's watching?"

"Over there on that little knoll. He's lying flat so he can't be seen. But he's watching everything you do."

"Is he now?"

She saw his face tighten and an ugly look come into his eyes. She had never seen this phase of him before, and suddenly she shivered, understanding that he might be a very tough customer in a fight. For a fight was what he had in mind quite obviously. She reached out and caught hold of his arm as he was turning from her.

"Jim, no. Don't do anything rash."

He halted to smile down at her, and now his smile was all for her, without any of that abstraction with which he had looked at her of late. He put his hand over hers where it rested on his arm, and his eyes were gentle.

"I'll be careful. Do you think I'd take a chance of getting hurt, when I have such a beautiful bride waiting for me? No, no. I'll be careful, all right."

He did not look as though he were being careful, however, as he went striding off toward that little mound where the man lay flat. To Betsy, he seemed very antagonistic and she noted that his big fists were clenched. The wind off The Wash ruffled his thick blond hair, and in her mind's eye he seemed like a big Viking clad in modern-day clothing.

MY TREASURE, MY LOVE

There was no movement on the hill for a few moments; then a man sprang to his feet and began to run. Betsy saw the man clearly now for the first time. He was small, with a shock of black hair framing his baldness and with a face that was burned by the sun. He wore old clothes that reminded her very much of the sort of clothing fishermen wore.

He ran swiftly, and Jim came to a stop and watched him race away.

"Just a local who wondered what we were doing," Jim said when he came back to her. "He probably thinks we're mad, driving a drill down in such ground."

Betsy put her eyes on Jim's face. It did not seem to her that he was regarding this intrusion in any such manner. There was worry in his eyes, she could see.

"Just be on your guard," she murmured.

His blue eyes twinkled. "Would it worry you if anything happened to me?"

"I wouldn't want anyone to get hurt."

He laughed softly, patting her hand.

He walked back toward the donkey engine and the drill, where Jason waited. She saw them talk together for a time before putting the drill down into the ground again and starting up the engine. She listened to its chug-a-chug for a time, then lost interest and began to walk once more.

After a time she began to get hungry. She felt that Jim and old Jason must feel the same, so she left the riverbank and walked toward them. They were bringing the drill up, and so she waited, standing close to them.

It was Jason who saw the bits of rotted wood caught in the drill.

"There," he exclaimed. "There's proof we're right on the spot. Look at that old wood. It's rotted, ready to crumble at a touch."

Jim was nodding. "Yes, I think you're right. We'll put her down again and let her churn a little more."

Seeing Betsy, he turned and held out the bits of wood for her inspection. "Parts of the wagon train—or so we hope. One of those wagons that held the gold is right under us."

Lynna Cooper

It looked like old wood to Betsy, nothing more. But she caught a little of their excitement; she took the tiny pieces from his palm and stared at them. If they were from one of the gold wagons, what a story they could tell! She could picture that story in her mind: the sweeping together of the waters, the overturning of the wagons, the screams of the horses caught in their harnesses. . . .

She asked, "Is anybody hungry?"

Jim turned toward her and smiled. "Now that's a sensible question. I'm half starved, and I suppose Jason is as well. Can you drive the Cobra and go bring us some sandwiches?"

"And hot coffee?" She laughed.

"Good girl. Here, take the keys. You can find a place in some village near here—Fosdyke or Moulton Seas End—where there must be a restaurant open. Do you have money?"

"Plenty." She nodded.

It was pleasant, sitting in the Shelby Cobra, driving over the narrow roads. It was as though she were driving through an empty land with the marshes all around her, and the fens. There was blue sky above and the flatland and the grasses waving in the sea breeze below. The road itself was narrow, hedged about by the fens. It was a lonely, remote spot, very much as it had been for the past thousand years and more, Betsy suspected.

As she came around a curve, she saw the man with black hair who had run from Jim Manners. He was standing at the edge of the road, bending to talk with a man seated behind the wheel of an ancient Humber. Coldness settled in Betsy, but she kept her foot on the gas.

The man turned as she came forward, and for a moment it seemed he did not intend to move. But the man in the car said something to him, and he stepped out of the way, giving her a hard look. She risked turning her head as the Cobra went by the Humber to get a look at the man at the wheel.

He was big, burly, with a straggly beard.

That was all she could be sure of as she drove past. She had no time for a longer look; the narrowness of

MY TREASURE, MY LOVE

the road and the strangeness of the Cobra in her hands demanded all her attention. She glanced into the rearview mirror as she moved along and saw that the man with black hair had resumed his spot, bending to talk with the man in the Humber.

Who were they? Why were they here, in this godforsaken spot? It had to do with Jason and his attempt to find that lost treasure. It had to be. This road was not a well-traveled one; anyone taking it would only land up at the edge of the river where it met The Wash. Peat cutters used it, of course, and fishermen. But except for those, it had no use at all.

She stopped at a hamlet, and in the local store she bought sliced ham and roast beef, a loaf of rye bread, mustard and mayonnaise. The woman behind the counter filled three big containers with coffee. While the woman busied herself with the order, Betsy chatted.

"Is the fishing good around The Wash?" she asked.

"Not anymore," the woman replied. "In my father's time it was better, and even better than that in my grandfather's. But today few men go there to fish, though some of them tell me the Welland still has fish in it, and the Glen."

"And the peat cutters? Are they still active?"

The woman smiled and shook her head. "Na, na. Not at this time of year. You'll not find them out there with their blades in this heat."

"It's lonely." Betsy smiled. "I was driving along and saw some men on the back road, the one that leads to The Wash. I just wondered."

The woman looked at her. "That's strange. They'd have no business there, unless they were sightseers."

"They certainly didn't look like sightseers."

"Probably got themselves lost."

With her purchases Betsy drove swiftly, but as she approached the spot where she had seen those two men, she slowed the car almost to a crawl. Suppose they had placed the Humber across that narrow dirt road? She would be forced to stop. Panic touched her for a moment, but she went on.

If Jim had been with her, she would not have been

so frightened. He had a way about him, he was confidence itself, and he imparted that confidence to those who were with him. She wished desperately, the nearer she came to the place where she had seen the Humber, that he was sitting beside her.

She rounded a curve and saw the empty road before her.

Relief went through her with her sigh. The Humber and the two men were gone. Her foot pressed harder on the gas pedal.

When she swerved to a stop, Jim came from the donkey engine to help her carry her packages. She told him about the men she had seen and the Humber. He listened quietly, his head to one side as his blue eyes studied her.

"Scared, weren't you?" he asked quietly.

"Well, a little. I pictured that car across the road and those two men waiting there for me."

"After this, I'll be the one to go for lunch."

That same glint was in his eyes, and she knew that if he had been the one who had gone for the food, he would have stopped the Cobra and, like as not, got himself embroiled in a fight.

"You be careful," she said lightly. "I don't want a banged-up husband."

"You could nurse me then," he said, chuckling. "That might be fun."

He put his free arm around her and squeezed her. His action brought her body up against his own, and she felt its hardness. She also felt the weakness of her knees at his touch, and a mental warning raced through her mind: *Watch it, girl! This guy is deadly*.

Jason shut off the donkey engine when he saw them and came to meet them, taking the packages from Betsy's arms and saying, "We'll eat on the bank, looking out over The Wash. It's very peaceful there, you'll love it."

When Jim told him what Betsy had seen, Jason Tilden scowled.

"I've been very careful," he muttered. "I haven't told any of the locals about what we were doing. No one at all."

"Well, somebody knows."

MY TREASURE, MY LOVE

"I don't like this, not at all."

"Not to worry. If somebody comes snooping around, I'll be only too happy to bloody their noses for them."

Jason chuckled, but it was without humor. "For what lies underground here, some men might be willing to play very rough. We'd best be careful about what we do—and say."

They ate their lunch side by side, with Jim sitting close to Betsy. For once, she was glad of his presence and did not resent his nearness. As though he sensed this, he sat even closer after a time so that their bodies were touching. Old Jason watched them, smiling.

Betsy gathered up the coffee containers and the bits of paper in which their sandwiches had been wrapped while the two men went back to the drill and the donkey engine. She sat and watched them, noting how easily Jim Manners moved about, all energy, very efficient. He took off his shirt after a time to work in the hot sunlight, and she saw the muscles of his back and front bulge and bunch when he had need to use them.

Again and again they put the drill down, apparently without any further success, and as the shadows lengthened along the ground, Betsy rose and went to join them. Old Jason looked very discouraged, but Jim was apparently still hopeful.

"One more try," he was saying to the older man as she came up. "Just one more, and this time I'm going to use that special drill I had made, the one I told you about in my last letter."

He moved to the Cobra, lifted out a case, and began opening it. The drill he brought into view had an opening between the bit and the shaft. He held it up in a hand and glanced from Jason to Betsy.

"I designed this baby, had it made to my own specifications."

"What's it do?" Jason Tilden asked.

"See this open part?" He tapped the section to which he referred. "If there's anything at all down there, this will catch it, bring it up. At least, I hope it will."

He moved to the drill head and removed the old drill,

fitting in the new. Betsy watched him for a moment before saying, "It's getting late, you know."

He nodded without looking at her. "Just this once. Then we'll go back, I promise. But I want to try her today."

The donkey engine throbbed. The drill bit into the ground, sank out of sight. Betsy waited, looking at the two men and thinking how much like boys they were, with a new toy. The throb of the engine seemed to be everywhere, entering into all their bodies.

She glanced around, wondering if those men were hidden somewhere, watching what was going on. She saw nothing but the sky and the peat fields and the distant fens. They seemed to be the only people in the world here.

"There," Jim was saying. "She's certainly deep enough now."

"Listen," Jason exclaimed. "She's making a different sound."

"I hear. We'll let her go on for a little longer and then bring her up."

They waited in the sound of the engine and the faint whirr of the drill before Jim said softly, "Okay. Time's up."

The drill came out of the ground slowly, then more swiftly. Betsy moved a step or two closer, seeing the chunks of dirt dropping from the rotating drill, her eyes waiting for that open section. Then it was before them.

Jim let out a yell.

Being closest to it, he could the most easily see what was contained in that opening. Yet Betsy herself had caught a glimpse of something yellow wedged into the mud in the drill opening.

Gold?

Chapter Five

She moved forward, crowding in against Jim, excitement all but choking her. Could it be? Was it possible that they had struck the site of the disaster of so long ago? She licked dry lips with the tip of her tongue.

"Is it? Is that really gold I see?" she asked breathlessly.

Jim turned and grinned down at her. "Looks like it, doesn't it? We'll have to scoop all that mud out first, to make sure. Now stand back, honey. Let me get this drill off."

She obeyed him, then stood and watched his back muscles bunch as he swung the drill to one side and began to loosen it. He worked easily, without haste, and it came to Betsy that he might be like that in all things. He did not seem to get excited, though certainly his heart must be slamming as hers was, his mouth must be as dry, he should be as eager.

She watched as water was poured over the catch basin, as the mud was washed away, and she heard the faint chink of metal, again and again. Too excited to pay any attention to anything but that gleam of gold, she crowded closer, edging her way in under his arm. She could see the coins now—three of them, bright and glistening in the rays of the setting sun.

"They are," she breathed, "old coins. Very old ones."

Jason Tilden was hopping about to one side of her, making gurgling sounds in his throat. He kept slapping his palms together as though he were applauding a spectacular feat. Well, it was spectacular, in a way. If they had found that lost treasure, they all were rich people.

"There," Jim said softly as the last of the mud washed away.

Little chips of gold gleamed here and there in the catch pan. But it was not these at which Betsy stared. Three round gold pieces, each stamped with an ancient sigil, gleamed there before her.

"Rose nobles," whispered old Jason. "In mint condition, too."

"Rose nobles?" wondered Betsy.

The older man laughed. "They didn't have pounds back in those old days, no paper money at all. The main coin was the penny. They made a gold penny after a time, back in the days of Henry the Second, but they were so fragile it was thought best to introduce new coinage.

"And so they made the florin, the noble, and the rose noble, the latter being the most valuable of them all." He drew a deep breath. "As collectors' items these three alone will be worth a good bit of cash. But think of the hoard that must be beneath our feet. It dazes me."

Jim bent, lifted a coin, and handed it to Betsy. She accepted it almost reverently. What a story this coin might tell! She studied the markings, the face of the man depicted there—Henry II?—and she felt a wild exultation sweep through her.

"We're all rich," she whispered.

"Indeed we are," Jason agreed.

Jim Manners chuckled. "Hey, you two. Don't start counting your chickens yet. We can't bring up that treasure with just this drill. We're going to have to dig down and do a lot of excavating before we can lay our hands on all the other gold pieces."

Jason Tilden made a long face. "That means sharing our discovery with other people. I don't like that, Jim."

Jim Manners laughed. "Do you think you and I can dig fifteen or twenty feet down? All by ourselves? Man, that's a backbreaking job for two men. We need a scoop shovel and plenty of men, a whole crew."

"I don't like that."

"But how do you expect to get at it?"

MY TREASURE, MY LOVE

"I'll have to think about it."

Betsy eyed him in dismay. Here she had gone along on faith; she had allowed herself to be married, expecting that as a result, she would share in a vast treasure. It wasn't fair.

She looked sideways at Jim, who was regarding the older man with a faint smile. How could he stand there so pleasantly and listen to this? Exasperated, she drew a deep breath.

"Do you mean to tell me that we aren't going to get the rest of the gold? It's there. This proves it." She held out her palm on which the gold noble rested. "There'll be thousands of such gold coins down there. Enough to keep us in luxury for the rest of our lives. And you stand here wondering whether to hire men and engines to get it up."

Jason muttered, "It isn't all that simple."

"Why not?"

He shook his head. "I must have time to think."

Betsy looked at Jim. He was picking up the other gold coins and handing them to her. She wiped them off with her handkerchief and placed them in her change purse.

Her mind was a swirl of doubts and indecisions. There was anger, too, and a sense of somehow being cheated. Very carefully she closed the snap of her purse and stood clinging to it, watching as Jim separated the tiny chips of gold and put them on a flat piece of wood.

How could he work so calmly? Didn't he resent this reticence of the old man? Had he come here to England to be held off and kept dangling on the will of a man old enough to be his father? Well, if he had, she hadn't!

"What do you mean, you must think about it?" she asked.

Jason's eyes slid sideways at her. He looked uneasy, almost guilty.

"Now, now," he said softly. "There's no reason to become excited. Naturally, we're going to do all we can to get that treasure. But I have to think about it."

"Why?"

She was aware that Jim had stopped what he was doing with those gold chips and had turned to look at her. Let him look. She was mad, and she didn't care who knew it.

65

Lynna Cooper

"I don't want all Lincolnshire traipsing here when we dig for that gold," Jason Tilden said. "They'll come at night when we aren't here, and they'll try to steal it away from us."

Betsy bit her lip, remembering that half-bald, unshaved man she had seen and the man in the Humber. There might be something in what Jason was saying. Still, he should have thought about all these problems before they started drilling. Or—

Did Jason Tilden really want that treasure?

Maybe he didn't honestly care about it, one way or the other. He had enough money to live on, or so it seemed. Why, then, had he gone to all the trouble of bringing her to England? Certainly, not just so she would marry Jim Manners.

That was absurd. Or was it?

She glowered first at Jason, then at Jim. Was Jim Manners in on this little plan to get her married to him? He hadn't seemed at all surprised when Jason Tilden made his request. Maybe the two of them were in cahoots.

And that was the silliest idea of all.

She was no heiress; she had no money. Jim Manners had never laid eyes on her before they had met at that inn in Cambridge. Oh, yes. He had seen her photograph. But no man in his right mind married a girl because he was smitten by her picture. Did he?

"You're crazy," she muttered, and moved away toward the Shelby Cobra.

She sat in the car and watched the two men cover the donkey engine and the drill. Jim lingered a moment to remove the drill head, then carried it to the car trunk and locked it away. Jason went with him, watching him with worried eyes.

Something troubled the older man. Could it be the fact that he was afraid someone else might come here and dig up his beloved treasure? Or was there some other reason for his inner fears?

They drove home in silence.

When Jim stopped the car, old Jason got out and walked toward the house, head bent. Betsy was about to follow him when Jim put a hand on her arm.

MY TREASURE, MY LOVE

"Let's drive around and eat out," he suggested.

"I'd like that," she said slowly.

What she really would have liked was to get some answers to the questions that swirled around in her head. She relaxed against the seat and nodded. "I'd like that, just a quiet dinner. But what about Jason? Oughtn't we invite him, too?"

"I did. He wouldn't come."

She waited until they were out of sight of the house before she asked, "Why is he so upset at the idea of hiring a crew of men to dig up that treasure?"

Jim took his eyes off the road for a brief moment to glance at her. "Jason Tilden is a very suspicious man. I suppose it's because of the sort of life he's led, digging up old artifacts in all corners of the world. A discovery of any great magnitude would make an archaeologist famous.

"So all archaeologists go to great lengths to conceal their discoveries until they can announce them to the world, with sufficient proofs to make certain that they'll get the credit for them. It's affected Jason, I think. He regards that treasure as he might the discovery of some proof that Atlantis really existed. He's afraid to breathe a word about what we're doing."

"But surely someone must have guessed! That man I saw today, for instance."

"Oh, I suppose so. It's hard to set about drilling for treasure in an out-of-the-way place like The Wash without attracting some attention."

"Well, for goodness sake! Didn't he think about that before he started? I would have. I'd have balanced risks and then decided either to go ahead or to forget about the whole thing."

"Jason had something else on his mind besides the treasure."

"Oh? What would that be?"

"Our marriage."

She swung about to face him. *"Our marriage?"*

"Sure. It meant a lot to him."

Betsy tossed her hands in the air. "I give up. I think the man is nuts."

"Just a born romantic, that's all. Who else but a born

67

romantic would go digging all his life for fossils or whatever it is that archaeologists dig for?"

"Why didn't he get married himself?"

"Probably too busy digging all the time."

An idea struck her, and her lower lip pouted. "Are you a romantic like that?"

"Sort of."

Betsy shook her head. "Marriage to me has always meant romance, I grant you. But getting married the way we did hasn't the slightest element of romance in it."

"You're kidding."

She turned again and regarded him. "You think there is?"

"I certainly do. Here we are, total strangers. Yet I fell in love with you just from seeing a photo of you. If that isn't romantic, will you tell me what is?"

"Love," she sneered.

"I mean it," he murmured quietly. "Ever since I saw that picture of you, I've been in love. You were something of which I'd always dreamed. A beautiful girl waiting somewhere just for me."

Betsy subsided. It was very difficult to be angry with someone who told you things like that. If only she could believe him! She threw a glance at him. He was not looking at her; he was concentrating on the road ahead.

There was a determined tilt to his chin, and his mouth was large but firm. All in all, she guessed he was rather handsome. In a manly way, that is. He certainly was big enough and strong. Any woman might find him very attractive and good husband material.

Any woman but herself, that is.

Now why was this? she asked herself. Was it because she had really had no choice in selecting him for a husband? If she had met him under different circumstances, and had he wooed her as might a lover, she might well have agreed to marry him. But this way! She had been told to wed him and that if she did not, there would be no treasure to be dug up and shared in.

Ah! Suppose this treasure were never found? Suppose old Jason would not permit the hiring of men and machines

MY TREASURE, MY LOVE

to dig up that fifteen feet of earth which kept the lost gold of King John forever from the sight of men?

She would have married in vain then.

"Here's the place," Jim said suddenly.

Betsy came out of her reverie to stare about at the glitter of white moonlight on water. A building was off to one side, its many windows lighted, its doors open, and she caught the fragrance of roasting beef. There were cars here, too, parked side by side, indicating that the place was fairly popular.

Jim Manners parked the Shelby Cobra and turned to her with a smile. "I used to come here many times when I was in England. I always came alone, but I always told myself that someday I would bring the woman I loved here. Come along now."

She went with him obediently, through the soft night with the fragrance of roses and honeysuckle all about her, toward the main door. Jim had taken her arm, was guiding her up the stairs and onto the wide porch. Then they were in a candlelit room, with dark timbers overhead and many tables crowded with men and women.

"This way," Jim said softly, and his hand on her arm guided her.

There was a little nook off to one side, the windows of which looked out over the waters of the Glen River. As she sat down, Betsy saw boats moored along the bank, some with their riding lights on. It was a peaceful scene; it seemed far removed from the excitements of the day.

"The roast beef is very good here," Jim said.

"Whatever you say."

"I wish you would always say that."

Betsy was surprised by his tone. "What?"

"I wish you would always say, 'Whatever you say.' It's a fine statement for a wife to make to her husband."

She sighed. "I'm not your wife. Not really."

"We must do something about that." He smiled.

"Oh, Jim. Please. Haven't we had enough trouble today? Enough excitement?"

"Oh. You mean that man you saw, the one who was watching us?"

She eyed him narrowly. "Doesn't the fact disturb you?"

"Not in the slightest.'"

"I must be a great coward then. Because all I can think about is trouble."

His hand reached for hers. "There'll be no trouble for you, Betsy. None at all. I promise that."

Almost against her will, she asked, "And for you? Will this trouble come to you?"

Jim Manners looked the surprise he felt. "I anticipate no trouble. None at all."

What she might have said then was never spoken, for the waitress came with the platters of steaming roast beef and Yorkshire pudding, and Betsy realized she was hungry. They ate by the light of the candle on their table, and for a time it seemed to her that they were alone in the world.

Yet some of her uneasiness was still inside her. As their plates were taken away and before the dessert and the coffee were served, she came back to what was plainly worrying her.

"That man," she murmured. "The one I saw today. Surely you know he was spying on us. Suppose he tried to find the treasure himself?"

"Well? Suppose he does?"

"Where does that leave us?" she snapped.

"Happily married, I trust." He grinned.

"You're impossible," she told him and devoted herself to the baked caramel.

But she had to admit that she was quite content, here with this husband of hers. His bigness, his quiet confidence filled her with a calm peacefulness. It was good to sit with him, to watch him eat, to study the lines of his face and the width of his shoulders. If only she could have loved him! Then life would have been almost impossibly wonderful.

She did not love him, however.

Still, she knew she was at ease with him. For the moment at least. He talked about their future in glowing terms, describing the sort of life they would lead. Betsy listened—what was the sense of telling him there was no future together for them—in something of a rapt daze,

MY TREASURE, MY LOVE

almost drowning herself in the word pictures his conversation painted for her.

After this treasure hunt in England they would fly back to the States so he could meet her family and she, his. Then they would take a plane for New Mexico, where he intended to construct a dam somewhere west of the Llano Estacado. She would be able to live in a fine hotel or, if she should decide, go with him to the dam site, where there would be a little cottage they could live in.

He talked and talked, and his words wove a shimmering veil of happiness around her into which she felt herself sinking. Their eyes stared into each other's, she felt swept up into his charm, and she knew that his hand was on hers, holding it and pressing it tenderly from time to time.

Only when he was paying the bill, removing pound notes from his wallet, did Betsy come back to the moment. Whee—oo! He had almost hypnotized her just then. She had lost herself in his words, letting those blue eyes envelop her, seem almost to hold her close.

Careful, Betsy. This guy is dynamite!

Yet when he caught her arm and brought her between the tables and out into the soft summer night, she went with him, not trying to pull free, just walking along in the sort of spell he seemed to have cast over her.

Even when his hand dropped from her and his arm went about her waist, drawing her even closer, she did not resist. She let him hold her so that their hips touched and moved together. She dreamed a little, understanding that if only this man and she were in love—in real love—she might be the happiest girl on the face of the earth.

Inside the car there was even more of that same strange intimacy between them. As the car began moving, he reached for her hand and held it on his thigh, gripping it with his own.

There was no harm in that, she assured herself. It was only her hand he was holding, after all. But the restrained power of his fingers as they squeezed her flesh from moment to moment, the sense of his bigness and his strength —all worked on her.

"Moonlight," he was saying. "Moonlight over The Wash."

Dreamily she asked, "What about it?"

"Don't you have a mad, crazy desire to see it?"

"We-ell. . . ."

His chuckle was soft. "Of course you do. And so do I. Do you know I used to drive to one spot that overlooks The Wash and sit there and yearn for you?"

"You did?"

"Many times. I'd take out your photo and talk to it. I'd pretend you were there with me; sometimes I'd even put your picture on the seat where you're sitting right now and hold a conversation with you."

"What did I say?"

"You were always contrary." His smile became laughter. "Honest Injun. You would argue with me, telling me what a nut I was and that people couldn't go around having crazy dreams all the time and then try to make them come true."

She smiled as if to secret thoughts. "I probably would have, you know. I'm an intensely practical person."

He was looking down into her face tenderly. "Do you think so? I don't, now that I've met you. I think that you're as romantic as I am myself."

She was still in the grip of that dreaminess which had held her for such a time. Here in the confines of the car, with the soft summer breezes blowing in on them through the opened windows, the rest of the world seemed far away. There was just the two of them.

And when he braked the car and turned off the ignition, she got out of the car and walked through the tall grasses with him toward a grassy knoll. Beyond them she could see the still waters of The Wash flooded with moonlight and could hear the soft lapping of waves below.

"Here," he said softly. "On this knoll. This is where I used to come and sit and dream of what you were like."

She sank down on the grass, folding her arms about her knees, staring at the water below, letting the silence and the beauty of the scene seep into her. He sat beside her, close enough so that she felt his body, but she did

MY TREASURE, MY LOVE

not move away. His arm went around her middle, held her lightly.

"Do you feel it?" he whispered.

"Mmmm. . . ."

"The stillness, the waves down there, the touch of moonlight on them, silvering them. There are places like this all over the world, but this is one of my favorites. A man can dream here, let his thoughts go, tell himself what it is he wants most in the world and even feel that he's going to get it."

It was a beautiful place, there was no denying that. And it appeared to work its magic on her, too. There was a softness in her, an unreality; it was as if she were in a dream. She swayed even closer to him, felt his arm tighten about her.

"Betsy."

She lifted her face to look at him.

He kissed her then, his mouth soft and gentle on her own, and her lips met his, gave of themselves. Her body pressed his; her every nerve leaped with pleasure. For a moment or two longer she gave of herself in that kiss. Her body strained to his; she felt her senses leap and go mad.

Just for an instant longer did she kiss him.

Then she was fighting him, pushing away and rising to her feet.

"You . . . you . . ." she panted.

He smiled up at her. "You love me, Betsy. Don't bother fighting it."

"Tha—that's ri—ridiculous!"

Ah, but was it? Of course it was! It had just been the moment, the knoll and the moonlight over The Wash. That was all. External influences against which she had not been on her guard.

She must fight this man. Not only this man, but her own body. Because her body wanted his body against her own, her lips wanted his mouth covering them. Just then, when he had kissed her, she had been swept up into a delight she had never known, had never imagined.

And that delight scared her.

He was saying softly, "It isn't at all ridiculous. You

Lynna Cooper

know that, deep inside you, even if you won't admit it. What is it about me you don't like?"

She turned away, staring over The Wash. Tears came into her eyes, and she blinked them away. There was a maelstrom within her, a twisting of emotions she had never before experienced.

"This—this is a business prop-proposition," she found herself saying. "Nothing more. To learn about that treasure, we had to get married. There's no love involved. There—there couldn't be."

Could there?

Well, of course not. Life wasn't like that. She knew enough about life to understand that. A man and a woman didn't just meet and fall head over heels in love, not in such a situation.

Jim Manners sighed, rose to his feet.

"Don't come near me," she yelled.

"Scared?"

Her ears caught the tenderness in his voice, and she rebelled against it. Oh, he was probably used to this, to getting a girl to fall for him. He probably had girls all over the world on whom he had used these same tactics. Dine them, talk to them in that seductive voice of his, give them a squeeze or two, take them to some romantic spot, and then they would drop into his arms like overripe fruit.

"Take me home," she whispered.

He held out his hand. "Friends?"

She glanced at him, saw his somber face.

"You probably think I'm some sort of nut," she muttered. "It's just that we aren't in love, and I don't want to—"

"What? Find out we are?"

She shook her head, staring down at her interlocked fingers. "We couldn't be. Things just don't work out that way."

"If you say so. But we can still be friends."

She glanced suspiciously at his outheld hand. Sighing, she put her hand in his, felt it squeezed.

"See? It didn't bite. Nor do I. Now you just come along. We'll get you tucked in bed so you can have a nice rest."

MY TREASURE, MY LOVE

He was treating her like a child. Hmm. Maybe she was being a little childish at that. Girls didn't act this way with men—especially men they were married to!—in this third quarter of the twentieth century. Never mind that. She did. And she was the only girl involved in this crazy situation.

They drove home in silence.

Jason Tilden was sitting on the back porch when they drove up. He came to meet them, walking through clouds of pipe smoke. His face seemed more lined; he even looked somewhat older.

"I've been sitting here thinking," he told them. "I don't like the idea of having someone spying on us. I think what we should do is take a break for a day or two."

"Why?" Jim asked bluntly. "The thing to do now is keep working with that drill until we're sure we're over that treasure. We may have just picked up a few spilled coins, you know. We may not be over the main treasure."

"I know that. Well, if you feel we should do some more drilling, all right. But I don't want to find out that we're going to have to stand off a gang of roughnecks."

Jim shook his head. "No fear of that. Even if we have to, I wouldn't mind a little brushup with them." He turned and glanced at Betsy. "You still have those coins we found today?"

"In my pocketbook."

"Take them tomorrow to a coin dealer I know in Boston. That's about five or six miles directly north of Fosdyke. Get an appraisal on them."

She nodded, then moved toward the house, leaving the men talking.

She wanted time to think, to go over what had happened to her this night. That kiss had really shaken her, back there at that rock. Her first impulse was to pass it off as a chance happening, but deep within her she felt it was something more than that.

Could it be that she had fallen for Jim Manners?

As, no doubt, a lot of other women had done?

She sneered at herself as she closed the bedroom door. She was little better than a young girl after her first date. Emotions stormed within her; she felt a little giddy and rather fearful. Would she be able to keep him at arm's length, as she intended? Her body was a traitress to her will. She had discovered that, all right, this evening.

She stared at herself in the bureau mirror. Her color was heightened, rather flushed, and her green eyes were brilliant. Her thick black hair was windblown, but it framed her features pleasantly enough. Betsy leaned close, eyeing her mouth. Were her lips swollen? From that kiss?

Or had there been more than one kiss?

She wasn't at all sure. The only thing she knew for certain was that she had returned his kiss—or kisses—just as eagerly as though she were really in love with the guy. And that would never do.

Betsy disrobed swiftly, slid into her print pajamas. She was doing up her hair when the door opened and Jim walked in. Betsy scowled, remembering how he was in the habit of running his eyes over her body when she was in her night attire.

"Couldn't you have waited" she snapped.

"What? And miss this intimate moment?"

"You're impossible," she muttered and moved toward the bed.

When she was beneath the covers, he began his own undressing. Betsy flopped over on her side and closed her eyes. She could hear him, however, as he moved about, and so she pulled the covers up over her ears.

"The bed looks very comfortable," he said suddenly.

She lay there without speaking for a moment. Then she murmured, "If you want to sleep in it, I'll use the sleeping bag."

"No, no. Wouldn't think of it."

The lights went out. She could hear him sliding into the sleeping bag, heard his sigh. Her eyelids closed. She tried to put out of her mind the thought that he was almost within touching distance. If he should get up during the night and decide that the bed was more comfortable than that bag he was in, there wasn't much she could do about it.

If she were awake, she would get up and slide into the bag.

MY TREASURE, MY LOVE

But if she were asleep?

She woke to bright sunshine pouring through the windows. She was warm and cozy; she didn't want to move. She lifted her head, remembering this husband of hers, but the room was oddly silent.

"You awake?" she called.

No answer. Betsy tossed back the coverlets and stood up. A glance at the sleeping bag told her it was empty. She ran for the bathroom and the shower.

The house was empty, she discovered when she went downstairs. There was a note from Jim.

> Dearest One:
> Out at the digs with Jason. Don't forget about those coins.
>
> Your adoring husband,
> Jim

Betsy snorted. "'Your adoring husband,'" she quoted. "Phooey."

But as she prepared her breakfast of soft-boiled eggs and toast, she began to smile. She had to admit—be honest with yourself, Betsy!—that Jim Manners was very much the way she would want her husband to be. Of course, he was always staring at her, but she supposed that was a mannish trait and to be expected. At least in a brand-new husband.

He had that inclination to be snatching at her and kissing her, too. Right on the mouth. She knew where he was hoping that would lead, she told herself darkly. But there was no chance of that if she stayed on her guard.

She missed his presence as she ate. Of course, that was silly of her, but it was a fact. She felt lonely suddenly. Was she becoming accustomed to having him around her all the time? Wasn't there some sort of song about that? She hummed a few bars, trying to remember the words.

The sunlight was gone when she walked out to the car, and overhead the clouds looked ominous.

She drove through the rain to Frampton and on to Wyberton. Just before she came into Wyberton, the rain stopped and the sun came out. The fields on either side of the road were covered with very green grass, that particular color being the effect of all the rain, she guessed. It was pleasant, driving her little Hillman. She had not a worry in the world.

Well, almost none. She had forgotten about that husband of hers. Still, on a day like this, and being by herself, she could ignore him. Time enough to worry about Jim Manners when she went back to Jason Tilden's house.

She parked her car and began to walk, her eyes caught by the Boston Stump, the great tower of St. Botolph's Church. It stood two hundred and seventy-two feet high and gave a view that extended for forty miles over the surrounding countryside. Betsy saw a plaque that stated that this noble tower had been restored to its former status by the generosity of the people of Boston, Massachusetts.

When she came to the store Jim Manners had suggested, she paused a moment to stare at the rare coins on display in the windows. There was no coin there, she noticed, nearly as rare as the three she carried in her purse.

Betsy walked inside and toward a glass counter. A man in his middle fifties, wearing pince-nez attached to a black ribbon, came toward her.

"May I help you?" he asked softly.

She smiled. "I hope so. I want to have a value put on three coins."

"Of course. May I see them?"

He pushed a square of black velvet across the glass countertop. Betsy opened her handbag, lifted out her handkerchief, and removed the three rose nobles. She put them down on the black velvet.

The man stared at them a moment, as though in disbelief. Then, as excitement got the better of him, his hands began to shake. To stop their trembling, he put them on the counter. Twice he cleared his throat before he could speak.

Betsy was aware that the door behind her was opening and that a woman was entering, approaching the counter. Betsy did not turn her head; she was more interested in observing the man as he eyed the coins.

"Where did you get them?" he asked hoarsely.

MY TREASURE, MY LOVE

She shook her head, but she smiled. "I'm afraid that must be my secret. Are they worth anything?"

"My dear girl! If these are what I think they are, each one is extremely valuable."

That was when the woman who had just entered turned and stared.

Chapter Six

The man behind the counter adjusted his pince-nez. Then he extended a hand and lifted one of the coins. He stared at it a long moment, then turned it over and regarded the obverse side.

"May I ask where—no, no. You've already refused to tell me. What I cannot understand is why they are in such condition. Almost mint."

"They've been hidden a long time," Betsy murmured.

The numismatist regarded her somberly. His fingers that held the coin were trembling. Betsy was afraid for an instant that he might be going to faint.

"They must indeed have been hidden," he said softly. "I have seen such coins, but never in such condition. Usually coins such as these are in the hands of wealthy collectors or in museums. But even museums do not possess rose nobles like these."

Betsy became wary. Was he implying that she had counterfeited them? Her chin came up, and her eyes narrowed.

"And their worth?" she asked softly.

"Thousands of pounds each, perhaps, if they are genuine."

The woman beside Betsy stirred slightly. She asked, "May I see one?"

Without waiting for permission, she lifted one of the nobles and examined it. Betsy turned to stare at her.

She was beautiful, with golden hair and pale-blue eyes

Lynna Cooper

and a skin that was all roses and cream. She was willowy, as tall as Betsy, and seemed to be very sure of herself.

"They are rose nobles, Miss Forrest," said the dealer.

The pale-blue eyes studied Betsy. They were cold eyes; it was as if she were being held up on a pin and examined. Then she was dismissed.

"Rose nobles," said the other girl very softly. "They date from the time of Henry the Second. A long while ago." She looked at the numismatist. "Could they be fakes?"

"Now listen!" Betsy snapped. "I didn't come here to be insulted."

She reached for the coin the girl held, snatched it from her fingers. Almost in the same motion she caught at the coin in the fingers of the dealer. She put both those coins with the other and began to gather up the handkerchief that held them. Anger was staining her cheeks a faint red.

The man began to protest, "Please, miss. I would like to examine those coins more carefully. They are worth a fortune, but I must be sure."

Betsy tucked the handkerchief into her handbag.

Almost too sweetly she murmured, "I refuse to stand here and be called a crook. Thank you and good day."

The numismatist was beside himself. He came around the glass counter and put out a hand as though to grasp her. He did not touch her, however, but his face pleaded.

"Miss, I beg you. Just let me examine those coins more closely. Wait. Wait inside. I'll take care of Miss Forrest and be with you in a few moments."

"No need for that," the other girl said. "I'll be back."

Those pale-blue eyes ran up and down Betsy, then slid away. She turned and walked from the store. Betsy told herself she was being silly, but she did not like that girl. Not at all.

She turned back to the counter when the door closed behind her and lifted out the handkerchief that held the coins. Once again she spread them on the counter. The numismatist was beside himself with eagerness. He rubbed his hands together, and his eyes glistened at sight of the rose nobles.

"I would like to spend a day looking them over," he was

MY TREASURE, MY LOVE

saying. "I have a friend who is very knowledgeable about such old coins. I would like him to see them, to give me his opinion. However. . . ."

He lifted a magnifying glass from his pocket and hunched over. One by one he lifted the coins and studied them, turning them over and over in his fingers. As Betsy watched him, she saw his face grow pale with suppressed excitement. When he lowered the coins into the handkerchief, his lips trembled.

He said, "They are genuine. I will swear it. Three rose nobles of King Henry. It cannot be."

"And their worth?"

His eyes returned from wherever they were staring to look at her. His smile was gentle.

"My dear young lady, I cannot even begin to give you a guess. Five thousand pounds? Ten? Twenty? Fifty? Who can say? I know collectors who would give their eyeteeth for such coins. But to let them know what we have, to let them examine them, to call in their own experts—all this will take time."

He drew a deep breath. "I assume you are willing to sell them?"

"I don't know. I . . . haven't decided." When she saw his disappointment, she explained, "I'll have to think about it. But I'll be back."

"I sincerely hope so. I do indeed."

Making certain that the coins were safely tucked away inside her purse, Betsy smiled and nodded, then turned toward the door. As she came out onto the sidewalk, she paused to stare around her, eyes roving for sight of the blond woman. She had not liked the way in which she had snatched at the rose noble or the manner in which her cold blue eyes had run over her. Anger still seethed inside her, but Betsy told herself to forget it.

The woman had been rude, inconsiderate. She had met some of that sort in the past. She moved toward where she had parked the Hillman.

She drove back toward Fosdyke slowly, her thoughts running around the three gold coins, the numismatist, and the blond woman. The numismatist had been suspicious of her, but perhaps she couldn't blame him for that. It was as

Lynna Cooper

though someone had walked into a rare book dealer with a hitherto-unknown folio of Shakespeare's works.

Thousands of pounds? Just for those three rose nobles? Even if they were in mint condition! Still, she had heard tales of collectors and what they would do and spend to get rare pieces for their collections. And now she began to worry. The three coins ought to be in a safe-deposit box in some bank, not just lying loose in her purse. She told herself to speak to Jim about this first thing.

Then she forgot about everything but the Lincolnshire countryside as she drove through it.

She was moving along a straightaway when she became conscious of a big silver car behind her, rapidly approaching. Her eyes touched the mirror again, as though to make certain of what she saw. Surely, that was a Rolls-Royce. A Rolls-Royce with silver paint.

What was it called? Of course. The Silver Cloud.

It cost in the neighborhood of sixty thousand dollars.

Whoever was behind the wheel must be very wealthy. Envy did not touch her, for such things as Rolls-Royces had never been much in her thoughts. She tried to catch a glimpse of the driver.

The car was very close now, swinging out to pass her. There was a blond woman behind the wheel. Betsy recognized her as the woman she had seen in the rare coin store.

Then the Rolls-Royce was sweeping past her.

She slid a glance sideways. There was no mistake. It was the same woman all right. For a moment, Betsy thought she meant to push her over and make her stop. But the car continued on; it was as though she and her little Hillman had not existed. In a few moments it was out of sight.

"Now where will she be going?" she murmured.

To see Jim Manners?

Now whatever had made her think that? There was nothing on which to base such an assumption. But Betsy had a gut feeling. That blond woman was the sort who would go for a man like Jim Manners. Haughty, sure of herself and her beauty, she was the kind to brush aside any other woman as no competition.

MY TREASURE, MY LOVE

Even a wife?

To her surprise, Betsy's foot had pressed down harder on the gas pedal, so that she was traveling faster and faster. She made herself relax with an effort of will; she slowed down and eased back to her more normal rate of speed. There was no point in rushing back.

Even if the blond woman were on her way to see Jim—assuming, of course, that she knew where to find him—there was little Betsy could do about it. But she felt a hot tide of resentment swell up inside her. After all, Jim Manners was her husband.

Oh, come on, Betsy Jane! Be honest with yourself.

Sure, sure. Jim was her legal husband. But he wasn't her husband. Not—not in actuality. Betsy frowned. She had no claim on him, on his love. If she wouldn't fall into his arms, maybe that other woman would.

She nibbled at her lip. It struck her suddenly that she did not want to relinquish Jim Manners to the blond woman. Especially to her! There was something about that one that sent a cold chill down her back.

Gone was her delight in the day. She brooded now and worried, as she sent the Hillman around curves and down the straightaways. Nor did she lift her eyes to the sides of the road, where the cows were, and the neat farmsteads. Her attention was always on the road ahead, even though her mind was inclined to wander.

What will you do, Betsy Jane, if that other woman is with Jim?

"Nothing," she muttered grumpily. "Absolutely nothing."

Foolish, foolish! You know very well no man in his right mind is going to pay much attention to a woman who keeps turning him off every time he shows the slightest spark of affection. How patient can you expect a guy to be? The Middle Ages, with their courts of love and all that jazz about unrequited love, were so much nonsense. Maybe it worked in those times, but not today.

She drove up the drive to the stone house, eyes searching for sight of the Silver Cloud. The only car she saw was the Shelby Cobra. A vast relief flooded through her, and her heart lightened.

Sliding from the car, she almost danced toward the front door. She saw the door open and Jim standing there, looking at her. Her feet carried her toward him, and her feet would not stop.

She walked right up to him and pressed herself against him, then gave him a hug.

"What's this?" he asked in surprise.

Her green eyes twinkled up at him. "Just glad to see you."

His arms were around her, pressing her tighter. "Okay, okay. What happened?"

He was really pressing her a little too intimately against his big body, but she did not feel like fighting to free herself. Instead, she gave him her widest smile and wrinkled her nose at him.

"We're rich. Or almost so. I thought you'd be happy to know."

His hug grew stronger. "Is that so now? Come in and tell us all about it. Jason's been on pins and needles all day long."

He did not free her, just stood holding her that way and smiling down into her eyes. She saw his blue eyes become a deeper blue, knew that he was feeling the curves of her body against his own. In another moment—

He did just what she was afraid he would do.

He kissed her, at first gently and then more strongly. Betsy told herself that she was playing with fire, even as she kissed him back. It wasn't fair to the guy to be sweet one moment and like a dash of vinegar in the mouth the next. She began to push him away.

To her surprise he let her go. Betsy was relieved but, at the same time, somewhat disturbed. If he really loved her, would he have let her push away so easily? He was far bigger than she, far stronger. He could have kept her there against him if he had wanted.

Still, he did turn her and, with his arm about her middle, brought her into the house, closing the door behind them. "Come tell Jason," he said softly.

Jason Tilden was standing in the living room, his white hair slightly awry, as though he had been running impatient fingers through it. His black eyes sparkled.

MY TREASURE, MY LOVE

"Well? What's the good news?" he asked.

Betsy laughed. "It's very good. I've rarely seen a man as excited as was that coin dealer. His hands actually shook when he handled these things."

She took out the handkerchief and the coins and spread them on the end table. They glittered there in the rays of the sun, almost as though there were something bright and sentient inside them.

"They're worth a fortune," she announced happily. "He wouldn't say just how much because he needs to have another opinion on them. And certain collectors will have to be contacted. But he assured me that they were very valuable."

Jason nodded, glancing at Jim. He said, "I've been listening to this man of yours all morning long and well into the afternoon. He wants us to go back to that site and begin working."

"Why not?" Betsy asked.

Jason murmured, "There may be trouble. Those men you saw. . . ."

Jim asked quietly, "Well, Jason, what about it? Do you have permission to try your hand at finding that lost treasure?"

"Of course," the older man answered indignantly. "I obtained the Crown's permission long ago, and it is still in effect."

"Then what's to stop us? Surely you don't believe those men Betsy saw are going to try to rush us and take away our gold?"

Jason rubbed his jaw thoughtfully. "The idea was in the back of my mind. I've dug for treasure before, and I've had to fight off thieves and robbers in the past. It isn't a pleasant business."

"But this isn't the wilds of Saudi Arabia or even the more remote areas of Turkey. There are police here, available at a moment's notice."

Jason Tilden gave his faint little smile. "Yes, you're right, I suppose. Maybe it's because I've become a lot older in the past few years. I find myself dreading things I would have taken in stride ten years ago."

He clapped his hands together. "Very well then. Tomorrow we begin work again. Who knows? We may have struck the exact spot where those treasure wagons went down. In that case we'll be able to dig right where we are and ask for police protection at the same time."

He was turning back to his chair when the doorbell clanged. Jason swung about, white eyebrows raised. "Now who could that be? I don't have callers."

Jim muttered, "I'll go see."

Betsy trailed him out into the hall. As he swung the door open, her heart lurched and she gasped.

The blond woman she had seen in the numismatist's shop was standing there. Even worse, she was brimming with secret mirth. She held out her hands to Jim, and there was laughter on her red mouth.

"Jim, darling! Why didn't you let me know you were in England, you naughty boy?"

Betsy stared, aware that something inside her was turning over with sickening slowness. So she had been right. This woman knew Jim. Knew him well enough to call him darling anyhow. And darling Jim was probably beaming right back at her.

"Glenna," he was saying. "Well, how are you? This is a real surprise."

Betsy saw her eyes move from Jim toward her. Just for a moment they lingered, then dismissed her. Then she was stepping forward, pushing herself against Jim and wrapping him in her arms.

They kissed.

Betsy drew a deep breath. She wanted to run forward and push them apart; she also wanted—very badly—to haul off and drive her palm against the pink cheeks of this woman. Rage flooded her, which surprised her.

After all, she didn't have any real call on Jim's loyalty or his love. She hadn't acted as a wife would act. She could scarcely blame him if he hugged and kissed this woman who seemed so delighted to see him.

She stood there—as her father might have said, like a bump on a log—while Jim and this blonde woman practically made love in front of her. Her eyes narrowed. Jim was certainly taking his time in pushing her away. Well,

88

MY TREASURE, MY LOVE

maybe she couldn't blame him for that, she told herself miserably.

She cleared her throat.

Maybe she recalled Jim to the moment, she decided; maybe she was reminding him that he did have a wife, after all. Because he lifted his hands away from the blonde, to catch her hands and raise them.

"I'd like to introduce my wife, Glenna," he muttered.

As though it hurt him to say the words!

"Your wife? Oh, Jim!"

There was a wealth of sorrow and dismay in her voice, Betsy realized. But was it sincere or mere playacting? The blonde turned then and stared at her, and once again Betsy felt she was being studied like an insect on a pin. She grew aware that she was not at her best; the drive in the Hillman had tousled her black hair, and she was wearing slacks and a sweater that seemed rumpled and worn before the cool elegance of this woman.

"Good afternoon," the blond woman said coolly.

Betsy nodded. "Good afternoon."

"I've seen you before somewhere. Haven't I?"

You know very well you've seen me. And where. But Betsy only smiled and gave a faint shrug to her shoulders. "It could be," she murmured.

Glenna Forrest was staring up at Jim with her big blue eyes. Sickening, Betsy told herself. She had been dismissed as though she did not exist. For a moment longer she watched these two, and then she turned and walked back into the living room, where Jason was sitting, staring out the window.

He lifted his head as she entered, asking, "Who is it, Betsy?"

"Some old flame of Jim's."

"Oh?" The older man frowned. "Not Glenna Forrest?"

"You know her?"

Jason Tilden smiled faintly. "Indeed I do. She's been after Jim a long time."

"Has she now?"

Something in her voice must have betrayed her because he turned to look up at her. Understanding lay in his face as he nodded.

"A long time, yes. But Jim has never paid too much attention to her."

"He was paying attention out in the hall."

Jason shook his head. "Not to worry. It doesn't mean a thing."

Betsy was not so sure about that. A man and a woman don't embrace and kiss in the way Jim and that blonde had and have it be a purely platonic thing. She was just about to turn away when Jim came in, guiding Glenna Forrest with a hand on her elbow.

As though that one needed help!

"Glenna's here, Jason. She saw Betsy in the coin store and came to see what it was all about."

Jason made a face. Betsy had her own features under control.

"A friend of mine gave me those coins," she said softly. "I was just curious to know if they were at all valuable."

Glenna Forrest ignored her, staring up at Jim. "Are you digging for that lost treasure, Jim? Have you and Jason finally decided to go ahead?"

Betsy sat appalled. How had she learned about the treasure?

Jim looked uncomfortable. He shrugged and said, "Just looking around. Nothing to get excited about."

"May I see the coins?" Glenna asked sweetly.

Jason looked at Jim, who seemed embarrassed. Betsy told herself that sooner or later, if she kept at it, this blonde was going to get a look at those rose nobles. So why put it off? She reached for her handbag.

"Okay," Jim said.

Betsy handed over the coins, then watched as Glenna Forrest walked toward a window, carrying them in a palm. She bent her head then, studying them. It seemed to the watching Betsy that her entire body was a symbol of greed. But that could scarcely be; after all, any girl who drove a Rolls-Royce Silver Cloud was not in need of money.

"They look genuine," she muttered after a long study. "They certainly are rose nobles all right. If I remember the pictures of them I've seen."

It was Jason who murmured, "They're rose nobles all right."

MY TREASURE, MY LOVE

The cold blue eyes settled on Jason. "Where did you find them?"

Betsy couldn't help it. The words just came out. She snapped, "That's our secret."

Glenna Forrest acted as though she had not heard her. She said again, "Where did you find them, Mr. Tilden? I asked you a question."

Jason smiled faintly. "As Betsy told you, Glenna, it's our secret. You can scarcely blame us for that, now can you?"

Glenna looked at Jim. "Jim, you can tell me."

Betsy waited, her heart in her mouth. Would he tell her? Would he?

Jim said gently, "My two partners have given you your answer, Glenna. It really is our secret and must remain so."

"You won't tell me?"

"Afraid not."

Her right hand, which held the coins, closed into a fist. It quivered. Betsy told herself that this one was inclined to get her own way in just about everything she wanted. Yet her face remained bland, almost without expression. Glenna Forrest sighed softly.

"I think you're being mean, all of you. I asked a simple question, and none of you has the courtesy to answer it."

The two men looked vaguely embarrassed, but Betsy tilted her chin. She did not like this woman, not at all.

And so she said, almost too sweetly, "If you were a courteous person, you would not have been so pushy as to keep insisting on an answer."

The blonde looked at her more fully now, and Betsy could read hate and fury in her gaze. It was almost like a blow. She wondered if Jim could see those eyes as she was seeing them.

"I'll keep one of these coins," Glenna Forrest said then. "Just as a souvenir."

Betsy gasped. She did not believe the sheer gall of this woman.

It was then that Jim said, "I think not, Glenna. Just hand them over."

For a moment Betsy thought she might be going to defy them all. She wavered, and in that moment of her hesita-

Lynna Cooper

tion, Jim stepped forward and lifted the coins off her palm. He came across the room, placed them in the handkerchief, knotted it after folding, and handed it to Betsy.

Glenna Forrest watched quietly, but Betsy felt the touching of her eyes as those eyes went over her. Gauging her as a rival? As a wife? As an opponent? Betsy fought to retain her composure, to appear completely at ease.

Aloud, Glenna said, almost gaily, "Oh, come on. Why all the long faces? Just because I showed some interest in what you were doing? Jim, you know me better than that."

Jason said softly, "What we're doing must remain a secret for a little longer. Surely you can understand that?"

"Of course I do, and I don't blame you in the slightest for not wanting word of whatever it is you three are doing to get out. I won't say a word. Truly, I won't."

Betsy thought she was lying in her teeth.

Yet she smiled around at them, as though there had been no unpleasantness. She looked longest at Jim and then moved to take his arm. "Come walk with me, Jim. Back to my car. I have to run now, to keep an appointment —but I'll be back."

She said it like a threat, Betsy told herself.

She glowered as she watched them walk from the room. What was there about the woman that so annoyed her? Well, for one thing, her attitude toward Jim. She acted as though she, not Betsy, were the wife. She had ignored her so obviously, that it seemed almost as if she wanted to make her angry.

Or maybe because she thought Betsy was so insignificant, there was no need to pay her any attention. Something rose up inside her at that thought. Insignificant, was she? She would show her.

She got to her feet and marched herself toward the door.

"Yes, Betsy. Go get him."

She turned in surprise, seeing Jason watching her. He nodded at her, murmuring, "Don't leave him too long with her. That woman is a she-wolf. She's shrewd and has absolutely no conscience. Jim, I'm sorry to say, is too much of a gentleman to be able to handle her."

MY TREASURE, MY LOVE

Betsy nodded once, then went out into the hall and toward the front door which was partially open. She put a hand on the door and looked out.

Glenna was standing very close to Jim, smiling up at him beguilingly, her hands on his forearms. It looked as though she meant to embrace him in another moment.

"Jim," Betsy called. "Jim, Jason wants to see you."

He jerked back, turning his head to stare at her. There was an expression on his face she could not read. But he nodded, spoke a few words to Glenna Forrest, and then walked toward Betsy.

Glenna stared after him a long moment, then moved to get into her car. She started the motor, then gunned it and drove away in a bit of dust even before Jim had reached the porch.

He asked softly, "Do you think I need a keeper?"

There was danger here, Betsy sensed. Had she hurt his male ego in some way?

"Jason asked me to come and get you," she told him.

"Him too," he muttered, almost angrily.

"I don't trust that woman, Jim," she said softly. "Neither does Jason. I'm sorry if that offends you because you seem to hit it off so well with her."

His eyes were almost as cold as hers. "I married you, didn't I?" he muttered, then swept past her to move into the house.

Betsy closed the door and followed him into the living room, where Jason was still sitting, fondling one of his pipes. There was a rigidity to Jim Manners' back that told Betsy how angry he was, as he came to a stop before Jason.

"Well, let's have it," he said loudly. "You sent Betsy after me; you must have had some reason."

Jason was very calm. His face, as he lifted it to look at Jim, was almost serene. "You know what sort of woman she is, Jim. She would have kept at you until you had told her anything she wanted to know."

"Would I? I get the feeling that although you seem to know what sort of woman Glenna Forrest is, you don't know very much about me."

"Don't I, Jim? I think I do."

Jim glanced at Betsy. To her surprise all the anger

93

drained out of him, even as he stared at her. He lifted his hands, spread them, then shrugged.

"You're too trusting, Jim. Always have been." Jason Tilden spoke as though he had never paused. "It's a good trait, but a dangerous one when you have something to hide."

"What've I got to hide? Unless you've made up your mind to start drilling again."

"I have. I thought you knew that before that woman arrived. Tomorrow we go to work, you and I. Betsy, too, if she's willing."

"Good. Then let's go find something to eat. We can talk over supper."

Dinner that night was not a great social success. The men talked, and Betsy listened. She was not concerned with the treasure, she told herself as she crumbled a bit of bread between her fingers. She was more distressed with Jim and his attitude toward that blond woman.

Not that I have any right to be, she acknowledged. If I were a real wife to Jim Manners—well! She had to smile, albeit somewhat wryly, at that notion. If she really were the loving wife she was supposed to be, she would be ranting and raving right about now. Or maybe even sooner.

No woman was going to hug and kiss her husband while she was standing by! Not even if she were a wife in name only. She was going to have to speak to him about that.

This very night, when they were alone.

MY TREASURE, MY LOVE

"No. I agree with you."

Surprised, she raised her eyes again. "You know that?"

"My dear little goose, of course I do. I've known it ever since I met her. But she intrigues me. I've never met anyone so self-centered. Everything she does, everything she says, has only one thought in mind. Herself and her wants."

"Oh. Then——"

He came across the room to sit beside her. His eyes were fastened on hers; she felt herself sinking into their blue depths. It was like losing all contact with the world around her.

"Then you have nothing to worry about. You or Jason. I have no intention of telling her about the treasure, where it is, what we've found. Nothing at all. Nor do I intend abandoning you to run off with her."

Her cheeks flared scarlet. "I didn't mean——"

His action cut off her words. He leaned forward and kissed her, his lips pressing down on her hungrily, forcefully, destroying all her will. She told herself she ought to fight him off, to thrust him back, but there was no strength in her, none at all.

To make matters worse, she kissed him back.

You did, Betsy Jane. You did!

His hands lifted to her bare arms, gripping them. She felt the strength of those hands, felt also the crazy impulse to surrender to them. She was drowning in sensations such as she had never known.

Then, abruptly, she slid sideways, away from him.

"Get away from me," she pleaded.

"For now, I will," he whispered.

She felt the bed move as he leaned closer until his body was almost across her own. Her heart thundered; her every muscle was as weak as water.

"But there will come a time," he went on softly, his mouth close to her ear under a tumbled lock of her black hair, "when I won't stop, when I won't go away. And you won't want me to, Betsy Jane. Don't ever forget that."

She shook her head to deny the truth of his words, but it was a very weak headshake. His hand touched her gently, for a moment, and then his weight was off the bed and he was moving away.

She lay in a welter of uneasy emotions. What did he mean, that sometime she wouldn't want him to go away? Did he think he was going to get her to yield to him just because he came near her or grabbed and kissed her? Ha! He didn't know her very well if he imagined that.

She settled herself more comfortably, still with her eyes closed and not daring to turn and look at him. Why, Betsy Jane? Are you afraid that if you turn and look at him and see the love shining in his eyes, you will melt? Is that it?

"Yes," she whispered to herself. "Yes, that's it."

Tears came into her eyes, and she bit down on her lip.

It took her a long time to fall asleep, even after Jim had turned out the lights and was in his sleeping bag. She had to be on her guard against Jim Manners. She must not let these intimate little scenes happen again. Not ever. Because she didn't have much trust in her willpower. Not after what had happened.

In the morning it was raining. Betsy saw the downpour through the windows as she dressed, and she fully expected that their expedition to the donkey engine would be called off for the day. But when she went downstairs, she discovered that Jason and Jim were all ready to drive to The Wash and work.

"You're crazy," she told them. "In this downpour?"

"There won't be anyone lurking around." Jason beamed. "We'll have the place to ourselves." He added, "You don't have to come, Betsy. It will be very uncomfortable there."

"If you two can go, I can, too," she mumbled, feeling like a martyr.

She regretted her decision two hours later, standing in the steady downpour, watching the donkey engine throb and the drill going down into the mud. Jason and Jim were ignoring the rain; they worked on as though the sun were out. She herself squished around in the mud, sitting miserably on a flat rock and staring out across the raindrop-dappled surface of The Wash.

She didn't even bother to look around for those men she had seen the other day. If they were crazy enough to lie in this wet grass and get pounded by that rain, why, let them. Nothing was worth this misery. Nothing. She turned and glowered at Jim and Jason, the throbbing donkey engine and the drill.

Crazy, that's what they were.

She offered to help them but was refused. It was at these times that she stared at Jason, listening to him cough, telling herself that he did not look too well. An old man like that should be indoors on such a day, not out here laboring side by side with a big, strong man like Jim Manners.

Betsy guessed the lust for gold did strange things to people.

They ate the lunch they had brought from the house, sitting in the car and listening to the drumming of the raindrops on the roof. From time to time she saw Jason Tilden shivering. Finally, she could stand it no longer.

"Haven't you two had enough?" she asked.

"Just a few more probes," Jim told her. "We've struck nothing, nothing at all. I'm getting the feeling those coins we found were just plain dumb lucky. The treasure's under here somewhere. But we must locate it before we can begin to dig."

She scowled at him. "Dig? In this weather?"

"No, no. We'll have to have a clear sky for that, or there will just be mud to get up. We'll change the site of the dig and try again."

"But not today."

Jim looked at the older man. "How about it, Jason? Want to quit work now?"

"Not on my account."

Betsy stared at him. His face was gray; there was torment in his eyes. He shivered again and then again, as she watched. He ought to be home in bed with a hot toddy in his hands, she told herself.

Aloud, she said, "You're driving too hard. Tomorrow will be a better time for drilling."

"Just a few more," Jim said. "Then we'll go."

Betsy sighed.

The afternoon was washed away under the driving rain. Betsy remained in the car for the most part. At least

Lynna Cooper

water didn't trickle down her neck in here, and through the steamy windows she could watch the two men at work. Twice she trudged out into the downpour, to remonstrate with Jim, pointing out that Jason was exhausted, that he was shivering.

Finally, Jim nodded. "Yes, I think you're right. I've overworked him."

"It isn't your fault. He could have quit at any time. It was his anxiety to find the treasure that was driving him."

"It drives us all."

"Not me," she muttered. "I'm tired of this treasure hunting."

She turned and trudged back to the car, aware that Jim was staring after her. She didn't care how she looked; she was annoyed by the rain, worried about Jason Tilden, and just about disgusted with everything. She got into the back seat of the car and sat there, glooming at the world through one of the windows.

Jason and Jim appeared to be arguing over something, she saw. Not angrily or with bitterness, but calmly and reasonably. Jason kept shaking his head; Jim kept insisting. Finally, Jason shrugged and moved away, toward the car.

When he got in, he was shivering steadily. It seemed to Betsy that she could hear his teeth chattering.

"You're old enough to know better," she murmured.

"I've never been sick a day in my life. It's just a little chill."

It was more than a chill, they learned after they had reached the house. He collapsed as he walked toward the front porch, and they had to lift him and half carry him.

Jim got him upstairs and into bed while Betsy phoned the doctor.

It took two hours for the doctor to arrive, dripping wet and in something of a temper. He was an older man, with gray hair and dark eyes, and he wore horn-rim glasses. His mouth was thin and turned down at the corners. He shed water in the downstairs hall as he removed his slicker, and he hunched his shoulders suddenly, as though water had slid down his back.

"What's the trouble?" he asked Betsy. "I've never been here before. Who's sick?"

MY TREASURE, MY LOVE

When Betsy explained, he looked furious. "Do you mean to tell me a man of his years was outside all day fiddling around with engines? In the rain?"

"I'm afraid so," Betsy muttered apologetically.

"Damn fool. Well, where is he?"

She led him upstairs and into Jason's bedroom. Jason was in bed, the covers up to his chin. He looked old and worn, she thought, as her eyes rested on him. The doctor growled something in his throat as he too looked; then he went and sat down on a chair that Jim had vacated.

Jim took Betsy's arm and drew her out into the hall. "I don't like the way he looks," he told her. "Not at all."

They waited in the big drawing room, neither of them speaking. Betsy could not sit still; she moved from one window to another, peering out at the downpour that never seemed to lessen. Jim tried to interest himself in an archaeology magazine, but it was a lost cause. From time to time he glanced at her; she was aware of his glances but paid them no heed.

When they heard the doctor coming downstairs, they both went to meet him, almost side by side. His face was grave, he looked worried.

"He's caught a bad chill, there's no doubt of that," Dr. Baines began. "If he doesn't catch pneumonia, I'll be extremely surprised. The man's resistance is at a low ebb. I'll be back first thing in the morning."

He moved to put on his raincoat. While he was getting into it, he said, "I've left two prescriptions on the night table in his room. Get them filled as soon as possible." His eyes became almost dreamy. "Even so, I'm not sure they can help him. The man's overextended himself. Man his age should be content to sit indoors on a day like this." He sighed. "I'll do the best I can, but I'm not promising much."

He stamped out, growling under his breath.

Betsy was frightened. She turned and looked at Jim, who was closing the door. "What are we going to do?" she whispered.

"Hope that the medicine works. I'll get the prescriptions, go into town for them."

"I'll sit with him then."

He was sleeping now, she saw as she entered the room and took the seat beside the bed. He looked so small, so gray! Her heart twisted in sympathy. For all his life Jason Tilden had worked in all sorts of weather at the various digs he had been on. In steaming heat, in lashing rain. Now, home again in England in the latter years of his life, he had acted as though he were still filled with the fires of youth.

If he should die. . . .

Betsy sat up straight, eyes wide with horror. He could not die. He could not! For that would mean she would be left alone with Jim Manners. It would mean the end of this playacting, this farce into which she had been cajoled to play a part. She would have to get a divorce and go back to the States.

Well, so what if she did? She had known all along she would do that, didn't she? This little adventure would be at an end. Betsy sighed.

Jason Tilden began to breathe hoarsely. She leaned forward, staring at him, wishing there were something she could do. Where was Jim? Why wasn't he back with the medicine? She felt as though Jason were dying right in front of her.

Tears came into her eyes. She felt very sorry for this old man, who had felt the need to turn to the children of his old friends for any romance in his life. She was not sorry she had done what he had asked, even though it was a false marriage. At least she had given him some happiness.

Then Jason Tilden breathed more easily, and Betsy relaxed.

There would be no drilling now for that treasure. Jason would take many days to recover his old strength. Indeed, it might be weeks before he was well again. By that time it would be September, and she would have to return to her teaching job.

Ah, and what of Jim Manners?

He can go off to Timbuktu, if he wants, to build them a dam or some such thing. I'll never see him again.

Strangely she did not like that idea, not at all.

That was when the doorbell chimed.

MY TREASURE, MY LOVE

She got to her feet and moved to the open door. Could that be Jim, back so soon? But he had a key to the house; he could let himself in. She ran down the stairs.

When she opened the door, she saw Glenna Forrest. She was immaculately clad in a white raincoat; there were white rubber rain shoes on her feet and a white hat perched atop her neatly coiffed blond hair.

"I'm here to see Jimmy," she announced.

"My husband isn't home."

She would have shut the door in her face except for the fact that Glenna Forrest had already begun to enter the hall. She did not look at Betsy but ran her eyes around the hallway.

"I can wait," she announced to the air around her.

"I think not. We have sickness in the house and—"

"Sickness? Who's sick?"

Anger crept up inside her, but she fought it down. What difference did it make to her if this woman was after her husband? Jim wasn't bound to her by any ties of love certainly. At the same time she was his wife. As far as this blond woman was concerned anyhow.

"Jason. He caught a cold. Now if you'll please leave, I'll go back to sit with him."

"I'd prefer to stay until Jimmy arrives."

"It isn't what you'd prefer, if you don't mind my saying so. Or even if you do. I have a very sick man upstairs. I want to be alone with him, to make certain he rests."

The pale-blue eyes looked at her. There was dislike in that cool stare, intense dislike. Well, she couldn't help that. Betsy wondered if her own eyes showed the same distaste.

She held the door open and smiled coldly. "If you don't mind?"

Or even if you do, she added to herself. Just get out!

Glenna Forrest gave a casual shrug. She stepped out the doorway and moved toward her car. Then she turned as Betsy was closing the door.

"I'll wait out here for Jimmy," she announced.

Betsy slammed the door.

Fury shook her as she moved toward the stairs. Normally she was inclined to like anyone she met. But this blond woman really put her back up. There was something about her she did not like. Not at all.

As she went into the sickroom, she heard another car and knew it would be Jim. She strode to the window and looked out. Glenna was talking to him, standing close beside him, and Jim was listening intently. It seemed to her that Glenna was pleading.

Betsy scowled. What could she be telling him? Obviously that his wife had been rude to her. That went without saying. But such a statement could scarcely take so long a time, nor would Glenna Forrest be so tense, so anxious. Was she trying to get him to divorce her and marry the blond woman? Probably, Betsy thought darkly.

Well, she could have him.

If she wanted Jim so badly, though, why hadn't she conned him into marrying her before now? It was a thought that made Betsy ponder. Hmmm. Maybe Jim wasn't as smitten with Glenna Forrest as she believed. Maybe he was simply too polite to get rid of her.

She turned from the window and went back to the chair.

In time—it was more than half an hour—Jim came into the room with the medicine. He smiled at her, then moved to the bed, standing there and staring down into that grayish face. His smile faded as he watched, to be replaced by a worried look.

"I don't like it," he said slowly. "He doesn't look at all good. I'm not even sure this medicine will help him, though we have to try it."

"Ought we wake him?"

"No, let him sleep. Sleep will help just as much as this stuff."

He sat down in an easy chair on the other side of the bed, and they spent the next hour like that, until Jason's eyelids quivered and he gave a little sigh. When he opened his eyes, he smiled weakly.

"I'm an awful lot of trouble. I'm an old fool who should have known better."

Jim said, "Now that you're awake, you'd better take this medicine."

After he had swallowed the pills, Betsy tucked in the covers about him, telling him to sleep. "It will do you just

MY TREASURE, MY LOVE

as much good as the medicine. We'll be here, within call. Want a bell or something?"

Jason shook his head. "No, I'll be fine. I feel all right, though weak."

She put her palm on his forehead. It was very hot. She glanced at Jim, who nodded worriedly. "You rest now, Jason," she murmured.

They walked out into the hall, and she closed the bedroom door behind them.

"Well? What do we do?"

"Sit tight," Jim answered. "What else?"

His hand on her arm turned her, brought her down the stairs. She was grateful for that hand; it was as though his strength were added to her own. The house was very still, very quiet around them, and Betsy thought that they were very much alone. It was almost as though Jason Tilden did not exist.

She turned at the bottom of the staircase and looked up at him. "What do we do now? Can we do anything to help him?"

"Nothing except see that he takes his medicine." Jim paused, looked worried. "I don't like his looks, Betsy. I've seen men with their faces as gray as his, and . . . they didn't last long."

She knew a moment of shock. If he died, then their little treasure hunt would be at an end. Ah, and what then? If she and Jim did not continue the search for King John's treasure, then they would each go their separate ways. And that would be an end to this marriage.

They spent the evening quietly, walking in the little garden behind the house after the rain had stopped, sitting on the stone bench, and talking in low tones. Betsy hesitated to bring up the subject; she fastened eagerly on whatever topic Jim mentioned, but always at the back of her mind was the same question.

If Jason died, how would it affect them?

Betsy sat with Jason until two in the morning, when Jim came in, having slept, telling her to go to bed. She tumbled into their room, got out of her clothes and into pajamas, and was asleep as soon as her body touched the bed.

Lynna Cooper

In the morning Jason was no better, though he slept on, waking only when it was time to take the medicine. Betsy cooked breakfast, which she and Jim ate in a pall of silence. She could not bring herself to talk about their marriage, not with Jason so sick. Something like that would have to wait.

Dr. Baines came and went, looking graver and more worried than ever. He shook his head to their questions, telling them that he did not like the way Jason looked, he had pneumonia, there would be a crisis—probably by tonight—but if he were to live, he would show signs of recovery by morning.

"*If* he lives?" she had whispered.

The doctor had turned his troubled eyes toward her.

"Jason Tilden is not a young man. His body is worn by the many years he spent in those hot countries, digging for artifacts. I am afraid he has not taken good care of himself.

"You've told me he was out in the rain all day, yesterday. He was soaked through. His body took a chill." Dr. Baines shook his head slowly. "Even a much younger man might be adversely affected. Keep me informed. I'll be right over if there's any change."

"He just sleeps," she whispered.

"Because his strength is gone. But if that rest and the medicines I gave him do their job, he'll be feeling better tomorrow morning."

When he left, Betsy had stood staring out at the winding drive for a long time. Not until Jim came up to her and touched her arm did she turn from that contemplation of the road.

"We must eat," Jim reminded her, a slow smile on his lips.

Now it was dinnertime, and the dreamy lethargy in which she had spent the day was still with her. She served the food and ate a little of it, though Jim pleaded with her to eat more.

"That wouldn't keep a bird alive, what you eat," he told her.

She smiled faintly. "I have no appetite," she whispered,

MY TREASURE, MY LOVE

and made a motion with her hand. "All day long I've been thinking."

Jim put down his fork. "Not pleasant thoughts either, judging by your face."

She would not look at him. "It's been . . . about us."

"I guessed as much. All right. What about us?"

"If Jason dies, that's an end of the treasure, isn't it? There's nothing to keep me here any longer."

"Hey, lady. You have a husband."

"Oh, Jim. Let's not play games, not when Jason isn't here to see and hear us."

His eyes were tender, going over her features, but since she was not looking at them, she did not see that tenderness. Yet she caught a hint of it in his voice.

"I'm not playing games with you, Betsy. I love you. I want you for my wife, treasure or no treasure."

Now she did look at him. "Why? Why could you possibly want me as a wife?"

"Damn it all, girl. I've told you I love you."

She shook her head. "You couldn't."

Jim sighed. He looked down at his plate, out the window, then across the table at her. "Do you want a divorce?"

Betsy hesitated. Actually, she didn't know what she wanted. She did not want to divorce him—was that because Glenna Forrest was there in the wings, so to speak, waiting to get her claws on him?—but she did not want a marriage with him either. She sighed again and shook her head.

"I'm a ninny, I guess. I don't know what I want."

"I do." Jim chuckled.

Startled, she stared at him. "You do?"

"Sure. You want to be romanced. But this is hardly the time for it, with old Jason upstairs dying. Just give me a chance, Betsy. That's all I ask. A chance."

She nodded, smiling faintly. "I am on a vacation. Even if—if we were to get divorced, I wouldn't leave England. I'd go for a little tour, until it was time for me to go back to the States."

"Fine. Just stay here, let me try and convince you I'm good husband material. What do you say?"

107

Lynna Cooper

His hand reached for hers, held it. His eyes held her own just as firmly as did his fingers. It was impossible for her to deny him. She found herself agreeing, even smiling as she did.

After all, here at Jason's house she would not have to pay any rent. She hated herself for being so mercenary, but she had learned long ago that a teacher had to count her pennies, she had none to waste.

They did the dishes together, and then they went upstairs to look in on Jason Tilden. He was still sleeping, but his breathing was becoming raspy. He looked smaller, almost shrunken, in the big bed.

"I don't like it, Jim. He—he seems to be weaker than ever."

"I'm going to phone Dr. Baines."

The doctor came at once and was with Jason for half an hour, sitting beside his bed, taking his pulse, studying him. His face was troubled; he plainly did not like the way his patient was responding. Finally, he beckoned to Betsy and Jim and took them out into the hall.

"He's sinking," he said. "Unless some sort of miracle occurs, he will die before morning. I'm sorry. There's absolutely nothing I can do. I've done everything humanly possible."

The doctor shrugged slightly. "I'll be happy to stay if you want me. If you have a couch or something on which I can lie down? I've been going ever since dawn, and I'm just about done in."

Betsy took him off to an adjoining room, leaving Jim with Jason. She made up a bed, gave the doctor a pair of Jim's pajamas. "You go to bed. You need your rest more than Jim or I do. We'll stay up and watch. If we think we need you, we'll call."

The doctor nodded. "The change has to come from himself; there's nothing more anyone else can do."

Jason Tilden died at five in the morning.

Betsy, who was half dozing in a chair, after having made Jim go to bed at three o'clock, was not aware of it at first. Only when she woke from a dream and stared around her did she realize that Jason was not breathing.

She went and bent over him. His eyes were closed; his

MY TREASURE, MY LOVE

face was white, pallid. Betsy whimpered, turned, and fled, racing into the bedroom where Jim was sleeping. Bending over, she shook him awake.

"I—I think he's dead," she wept.

He nodded. "I'll go fetch the doctor."

After that, it was chaos.

There were the funeral arrangements to be seen to, the family mausoleum was to be opened, Jim wanted to see Jason's solicitor, and the newspapers had to be notified. Betsy worked steadily; she was on the phone calling here and there, until toward midafternoon she told Jim she was exhausted.

He nodded sympathetically. "You march yourself upstairs and into bed. I can handle the rest myself. Go on now. Go."

She slept until the following dawn.

The house was still when she woke, there was the patter of rain on the windows, and to her surprise, Jim was not in his sleeping bag at the foot of her bed.

She rose and dressed, went downstairs. Someone was moving about in the kitchen. Jim, of course, she told herself, and went to greet him.

"I'm sorry," she began. "I slept so much that—"

Her words broke off in astonishment.

Glenna Forrest was standing at the sink, washing dishes. She turned and gave Betsy a cool look. Without a word she turned back to the hot water and the dishes.

"What are you doing here?" Betsy asked.

"Helping, of course. Jim needs me."

Betsy was about to retort when she realized that she had no authority in this house. If Jim had invited Glenna to stay and help, there was absolutely nothing she could do about it. She heated the coffee, poured herself a cup, and carried it into the dining room.

She was half starving, she'd eaten little enough yesterday, but she was not about to cook herself a breakfast with that woman standing by and watching her. She would wait until Jim appeared and took her off with him.

Hmmm. Where was Jim?

She sipped the coffee and waited. Not until she was

Lynna Cooper

just about finished did he drive up before the house. Betsy saw his red Shelby Cobra, went to meet him.

"What's that woman doing here?" she asked.

He eyed her blankly. "What woman?"

"That girlfriend of yours, that Glenna Forrest!"

His arms were full of packages. He put them down on the hall table, then scowled at her. "Glenna? Is she here?"

"Out in the kitchen, washing your breakfast dishes."

"Is she now?" he asked softly.

Betsy caught her breath at the look in his eyes. There was anger there, and—laughter. Was the anger at her? Or the laughter? She was turning away when he reached out and caught her arm.

"Have any trouble with her?" he asked.

"No trouble. I simply got myself a cup of coffee and drank it. But get her out of here, Jim. I want my breakfast. I hardly ate yesterday and—oh! What about the funeral arrangements?"

"All made. Tell you about them later. I want to see Glenna."

She trailed after him, wondering whether she should. After all, she had no call on Jim's love or loyalty. Still, she was his wife, if only in name.

"Well, now," Jim said as he walked into the kitchen. "This is a surprise."

Glenna Forrest turned from the sink, where she had been drying the dishes, to smile at him. "Darling. Hello. I thought I'd make myself useful while I waited for you."

"How'd you get in?"

Glenna Forrest opened her eyes wide. "The door was unlocked, so I just came on in. I saw your dirty dishes and washed them, as a wife ought to do."

"You aren't my wife, Glenna."

She shrugged and glanced past him at Betsy, waiting in the doorway. "If your wife doesn't do her job, you can't blame me."

"Look. Jason Tilden died early yesterday morning. We're up to our ears in funeral arrangements and suchlike. We—"

"Jason Tilden died? But that means you won't be hunting for that gold, doesn't it?"

MY TREASURE, MY LOVE

"We haven't decided."

"But you must have some idea. Honestly now, Jim."

Betsy saw the muscles in Jim's back relax. Almost a note of amusement came into his voice as he said, "We may go back, at that. We did find those gold pieces, you know."

Betsy wanted to cry out a warning. He mustn't tell this woman about that! If she could be sure that they had uncovered those rose nobles where they had been drilling, she would hire men herself and begin to drill after getting the necessary permission. Betsy was positive of this; she could almost read her mind through those cold blue eyes of hers.

Jim was talking again. "There's a fantastic amount of gold down there, as I suppose you know. At least a million pounds, considering its historical value. Then there's the Matilda crown and Tristram's sword. Can you imagine their worth to a collector?"

Betsy stared at him. Had he gone off his rocker? It was like waving a red flag in front of an angry bull. Glenna Forrest was all but licking her painted mouth.

"A million pounds?" Glenna breathed.

"Oh, at least that much. Did you know what that coin dealer told Betsy here when she showed him those rose nobles? Each one was worth thousands of pounds. Of course, if we find the entire treasure, the individual value of each coin will go down obviously. But there're so many of them in that ground that their total worth will probably be about a million pounds."

Glenna reached for a towel and wiped her hands. She was thinking hard, Betsy saw, and the greed in her pale-blue eyes had not lessened. After a moment she said, "I think I'll run along now, Jim. I—I have things to do."

"Of course." He nodded agreeably.

Betsy was beside herself with fury. Had the man lost what wits he had, to tell their secret to this woman? Didn't he realize that she would be after that treasure, too? They would have to race against time now, to find that treasure before Glenna Forrest discovered it.

Glenna was moving past her, she stood aside to let her go, and Jim went after her. Betsy glanced at Jim's

111

Lynna Cooper

face, saw a faint smile hovering there. But when Glenna turned to glance back him, the smile was gone. Betsy scowled.

Jim was not a stupid man. It was almost as though he had gone into that kitchen to tell Glenna Forrest all about the treasure. But why? What purpose could he have in mind? Didn't he realize that Glenna Forrest would make a try for it? Did he want her to find it, for some reason she was unable to understand?

Well, at least she was leaving.

And she wasn't bothering to linger either. She had what she had come here for in the first place some days ago. Betsy stood and watched the Silver Cloud move down the drive and out of sight.

Jim turned toward her and winked.

Betsy gaped. Then she asked, "Do you have all your marbles? Or don't you realize that all she ever wanted here was that treasure?"

"Let her look for it."

Betsy opened her mouth, closed it. "Wha-what does that mean?"

His hand caught her by the elbow, turned her. "Aren't you hungry? You didn't eat much yesterday. Come along now. I'll whip you up some scrambled eggs."

"You will? Can you cook?"

"Watch and see. I'll use the old family recipe. Come on now. Just do what I say for once in your life."

Intrigued, she went with him and sat at the kitchen table as he busied himself with a bowl into which he broke two eggs, adding bits of sliced ham and chopped peppers. He whipped up the mixture, then dropped it into a frying pan liberally coated with melted butter. Once in a while he would glance at her, to make sure she was observing him.

Abruptly he murmured, "I do hope you're taking all this in. This is an old family recipe, and since you're one of the family now, I think you ought to know about it."

Betsy merely sniffed.

But when he set the concoction before her and she

MY TREASURE, MY LOVE

tasted it, she realized that never before had she enjoyed such a breakfast. There was toast, golden brown and buttered, a fresh pot of coffee. Betsy ate it all.

He sat across from her, watching her carefully. When she was done and was complimenting him on his culinary skills, he brushed aside her praise. "I've had to fend for myself all over the world. You learn very quickly to cook well when you have to eat your own cooking all the time. Now about your new clothes. . . ."

"What new clothes?"

"A black dress and accessories. For the funeral."

"Oh!"

"We're his family, you know. So to speak, at least. He hasn't anyone else. I've been to see his family lawyer. I saw a copy of the will."

He waited as if waiting for her to speak. When she did not, he asked, "Aren't you interested in hearing about it?"

Betsy was surprised. "Why should I be?"

He smiled gently. "You're so different from Glenna Forrest, I find it hard to believe you're real. Well, he left everything to us, of course, always assuming we were married. Which we are. And so we inherit."

Betsy rested her chin on her fist. "All right," she murmured. "I can tell you're dying for me to ask. How much do we inherit?"

"There's this house, first of all. It now belongs to us both. It must be worth a small fortune on the open market, Jason always kept it in good repair, and he's done a lot with the grounds. The lawyer seemed to think it would bring in at least thirty thousand pounds."

"Wow," Betsy said, sitting up.

"Then there are his bank accounts."

Betsy blinked. "His bank accounts? But of course. The man was retired; he had to live on something."

"More than a hundred thousand pounds, all told. That isn't hay, honey."

"I'd rather have him alive," she muttered.

"And so would I. But the lawyer told me that since Jason always looked on us as his children and since he

113

had no other relatives, it was only normal for him to leave everything to us."

A thought touched Betsy's mind. She would gladly have exchanged all that money—if she could be unmarried.

Or would she?

Chapter Eight

It rained two days later, when they buried Jason Tilden.

Betsy stood close beside Jim at the grave, under his umbrella, watching the coffin lowered gently into the ground. Tears were in her eyes. She had not known Jason Tilden very long, but he had been a mild and gentle man, more a scholar than anything else, despite the digs he had made, and he had been thinking not of himself but of how much the treasure would mean to Jim and to her when he had caught that chill.

The coffin was deep in the ground now.

She turned and looked up at Jim. His face was grave; his eyes were sad. He saw the tears in her own eyes, and his arm went around her to hug her. There were few mourners at the grave. Honor Furlong was there, of course, sobbing softly, and there were two older men, men with whom Jason had been wont to play chess at times. But they were all.

Jim turned her, brought her to the limousine they had hired to carry them behind the car which had borne the casket. The chauffeur was there, opening the door. Jim folded the umbrella and got in beside her.

"It's all over," she said softly, staring straight ahead.

He glanced at her, startled. "What's all over? Oh, you mean Jason's life? Well, it was a good life. He did everything he wanted to do, and then some. His name is famous throughout the world as an archaeologist; he could have lectured at Cambridge if he'd wanted. He preferred to come out here and stay, just taking care of his house and its grounds."

"I didn't mean that," Betsy murmured.

"Oh? What did you mean then?"

"Us. Our marriage. It's all over."

Startled, he looked down at her. "Hey, you don't mean that."

"Oh, Jim, be sensible. It was a quixotic thing to do, admit it. There was no basis for our marriage, other than my greed to share in a treasure."

"Well, now. I wouldn't say that. Don't forget, I fell in love with that picture of you. If I could do that, isn't it easy to admit that I fell in love with you—the real you?"

Her lips curved into a smile. "It's nice of you to say, and I admit it does something to my female vanity, but as for actual love, well, I just can't go along."

"So what do you intend to do?"

There was something in his voice—sadness? despair?—that made her turn to look at him. He was staring out the window at the rainy fields past which they moved. Something tugged at her heart, seeing him that way, and involuntarily her hand went out to hold his.

"Oh, come on. Let's face reality, Jim. It was a romantic idea, sure. I admit that. But—"

"No buts," he said suddenly. "I won't listen to them. You don't mean to run back to the States, do you?"

He turned and looked at her, and she shook her head, her eyes caught by his. "No. I'm going to stay on in England, do a little traveling as long as my money holds out."

"Then why not stay here, at your own home? All right, with me. I won't touch you; you don't have to worry about that." Could that be bitterness in his voice? "I'll be just as circumspect as you want me to be. But we could have fun together, eat in quaint little places, have some fun together. It'll be better than doing things like that on your lonesome."

"That's true."

"Then how about it? Just stay on for a while, pick up our lives the way they were before Jason died—and we'll see what happens."

Her head told her not to yield, that it would be better

MY TREASURE, MY LOVE

to run away from here, to put her things into the Hillman and just drive off, out of Jim Manners' life. Ah, but something else fought against that decision. Her heart? She scoffed at that but found she was nodding her head.

"Why not?" she asked lightly. "What've I got to lose?"

Now his hand was holding hers, and she let him hold it all the way to the house.

The next day was as pleasant as the former had been rainy. The sun was out, it was cool enough to be very pleasant, and when Jim announced he was going to the donkey engine and try for some more of the treasure, Betsy nodded and said she would pack a lunch and go with him.

It was pleasant, working with him, she realized as she helped carry the drill and aided him in attaching it. She worked quietly; but she did everything that was needed, and she realized that she had watched Jason as he worked and had learned from him.

Once Jim paused to wipe his sweating forehead and to grin down at her. "You're a good worker," he told her. "I don't have to be forever explaining what to do to you."

She felt inordinately pleased and began to work even harder.

They found nothing, however, and Jim muttered that their earlier strike of gold coins must have been dumb luck. "But it's down there, all right. The trouble is, you'd need a whole company of engineers and diggers to get at it."

"We could hire them, I suppose."

His broad shoulders lifted in a shrug. "It might be money just thrown away. No, we'll make our try, and if we don't strike the treasure—at least we've had some exercise."

They worked well together during the next few days; they laughed at little mishaps; they waited together breathlessly for the drill to come up; they washed the mud from the catch basin side by side. It occurred to Betsy that she didn't care whether they found that gold or not—not really, that is—because she did enjoy being out in the open and working with the drill and donkey engine. Besides, they were always together.

Lynna Cooper

Afterward, when they had showered and dressed back at the house, Jim had another restaurant to visit for their evening meal. They were tired, relaxed, at those dinners; they enjoyed each mouthful of their food; they took time to laugh at some of the misadventures of the day.

For a full week they went to the donkey engine. Then Jim declared a holiday, on the eighth day, while they were at breakfast.

"No work today. We've earned some time off. It's too hot to work anyhow. Do you have a bathing suit?"

She nodded slowly, remembering the bikini she had tossed into her bag. "Ye-es, but—"

"Put it on. I'll wear my swim trunks. We'll pack a picnic lunch and be off. And leave the breakfast dishes. We can do them when we get back."

In the bedroom Betsy slipped out of her clothes and into the bikini. Frowning, she stared at it in something close to dismay. Those two tiny bits of white cloth didn't do much to cover her figure. If he wanted to look, he could see just about all of her. Ha! *If* he wanted to look! He did little else these days except stare at her; he always had.

She thought about removing the bikini and donning her slacks and a shirt, then decided against it. The days had been hot, this day promised to be another scorcher, and the idea of cool water around her was very pleasant. She snatched up a terry-cloth robe and flung it about her. Her hair she did not do up but allowed to fall down below her shoulders.

Jim ran his eyes over her, nodding, when she appeared. "I know just the place to go," he whispered, taking her arm. "It's a little cove a few miles from here; I think it's a tributary of the Glen. Now come along. I'll carry the lunch basket."

As they were about to enter the Shelby Cobra, Betsy caught movement out of the corners of her eyes and straightened. The Silver Cloud was easing along the driveway, slowing to a stop. And Glenna Forrest was reaching out the window, waving a hand.

"Hi, there. Just thought I'd stop by."

Jim muttered something under his breath and went to

MY TREASURE, MY LOVE

meet her. Betsy watched him, big and muscular, and a voice began to whisper in her head.

"Don't just stand there, girl. Go after him."

She trailed after him in time to overhear Jim say, "We're knocking off for the day. Taking a vacation."

"Oh, how nice. Then I won't keep you, Jim. You go ahead and have fun."

The motor of the Rolls-Royce picked up power and slid past the red car, moving off down the drive. Betsy turned to watch it.

"Now what was that all about?" he was asking.

Betsy was surprised. "She didn't want to hold us up."

His blue eyes laughed down at her. "Does that sound like Glenna Forrest to you?"

"Well, no. But she did leave, didn't she?"

"And I wonder why. Oh, well. No matter. Let's go."

They drove through the sunlight toward the Glen. Jim used the back roads, little more than lanes, until they came to a tiny strip of sandy beach beside the river. He parked and ran his eyes over it.

"Used to come here for a swim every now and then. It's so quiet, so peaceful, I fell in love with it. And I vowed I'd come back someday—with you."

"Well, here I am."

They spread a blanket on the grass and lazed in the sun for a time. Betsy was dubious about whether to take off her robe, but the sun was so hot she decided that she would rather be stared at than suffocate. As the robe came off, Jim gave her a quick glance, then averted his eyes.

Betsy was so surprised she stared at him. This wasn't like him at all! His normal procedure was to let those blue eyes soak her up, almost as though his brain were taking a picture. What was the matter with him?

He lay down on the blanket and closed his eyes. Betsy eyed him a moment longer, then dropped beside him. There was nothing wrong with her suit; she had checked that with a quick glance. Everything was in place. Why then, his sudden—what? Shyness? She could not believe that.

They came close to sleeping, there with the sun beating down on them, and it was Jim who finally rose and suggested a swim. Betsy rose to her feet and walked with him to the river's edge.

The water was cold but invigorating. They swam side by side, then floated.

Jim said, "I've been thinking about Glenna."

A coldness came into Betsy. "You have?"

Had he decided that Glenna Forrest was the woman he loved? Was he about to tell her he was willing to get a divorce? Her heart began to hammer. Oh, yes. She had talked about divorce, but secretly—deep down inside her—she knew that she did not want to divorce this man.

"Why did she run off so fast?"

Betsy paddled into position so she could watch his face. "She didn't want to interfere with our day."

"Ha. You believe that?"

"Not really, I guess. But why else would she leave so suddenly?"

"Because she wanted to get to the donkey engine, to use the drill perhaps. Oh, she wouldn't do it by herself. She'd have men at hand to do the work."

"Oh, Jim. You can't believe that."

"I can't, hey? You don't know that woman."

"What are we going to do about it?"

"Nothing at the moment."

His blue eyes smiled at her, and she felt the impact of his stare. She was very glad that the water was hiding all of her below her neck right then. Even so, she felt the flush rise from her throat into her face.

She turned suddenly and began to swim toward shore. Jim was following behind her. She must get to her robe and slip it on before he could touch her. If he should catch her and put his arms around her before she had it on, there was no telling what might happen.

She felt ooze beneath her feet and stood up. At almost the same moment she felt the nippers at her toe. She yelped and dodged sideways, trying to shake off the crab or whatever it was.

It released her just as Jim's arms went around her.

"I have you," his rich voice whispered in her ear.

Those arms held her firmly, pressed up against him. Her bikini and his swimsuit did not cover them very much.

MY TREASURE, MY LOVE

Betsy turned her face up to his, to protest against his holding her so tightly.

That was when he kissed her.

She melted against him. She just couldn't help it. No matter how much her brain protested, her body reacted. And for a few moments they were the only people in the world. The kiss was shattering to everything she had always believed. And her arms were betraying her as well. They lifted to wrap themselves about him and hold him just as tightly as he was holding her.

She did not know how long that kiss went on. Too long. And yet not long enough.

When his arms finally released her, she could not look at him. Blushing, covered by confusion, she waded blindly toward shore. If he should come after her, if he were to wrap those arms of his around her again, she would not be able to fight him off. She knew this and hated herself for her weakness.

She was reaching blindly for the robe when his hand caught her.

"No. Leave it be."

Betsy trembled, hating herself for her weakness. "I think it best that I do," she murmured softly.

"I won't touch you again. Promise. And you know you'll swelter in that thing."

She released the robe to sink down onto the blanket. She didn't dare look at him; she knew what he would see in her eyes. Twice she tried to talk before words would come to her.

"You see, that's why I think we should get a divorce," she managed to say at last. "It—it isn't fair to you, this marriage of ours."

"Stop worrying about me so much. If I'm content, you should be, too."

Her foot kicked at the blanket. "Nothing like—like that must ever happen again."

"Of course not."

She turned her head to glare at him. Was he laughing at her? No, his face was sober enough. But those blue eyes of his were screaming hysterically. She could not withstand their merriment, and her lips twitched into a smile.

Lynna Cooper

"It was just something that happened," she murmured.

"Like magic," he said, nodding.

"Jim, will you be serious?"

"How can I be serious when I know that you love me just as much as I love you? And that's plenty, believe me."

"I don't. I don't at all."

"You're just afraid to admit it to yourself."

Was she afraid? Oh, that was nonsense. But there was something inside her that responded to this man. Animal craving? Of course. That must be it. They were human beings; they had been in close proximity; it was only natural that they should respond to each other.

"You hungry?" he asked suddenly.

She was hungry, now that he mentioned it. She reached for the box with the sandwiches even as he gripped the thermos bottle that held the cold lemonade.

They ate side by side, staring out at the water. There was a strange contentment in her, Betsy realized. It felt very natural to sit here beside this man and munch on food even after what had happened.

So the guy kissed you. Big deal. You've been kissed before, Betsy Jane. Ah, but never like that. Never! The effects of that kiss still haven't left your body.

My body. Pooh! A lot it knows.

Betsy slid her eyes sideways at Jim, to find that he was grinning at her. "I suppose you feel quite proud of yourself," she muttered.

"I'm just waiting, is all."

"Waiting for what?" she inquired suspiciously.

"For the truth to dawn on you."

"What truth?"

He reached out so suddenly that she had no chance to evade him. His hands closed on her arm and pulled her down on the blanket, flat on her back. He leaned over her, blue eyes gentle as his smile, and then he began to kiss her forehead, her nose, her cheeks.

"In time it will come to you that you love me," he was whispering. "Until it does, I'm just going to be patient. Very patient."

With each word he spoke, he implanted a kiss somewhere on her skin. On her ear, her throat, her shoulder.

MY TREASURE, MY LOVE

She lay there quivering, unable to move a muscle, just waiting until he was through.

When he stopped, he stared down into her eyes. She stared back at him, and that was a mistake. She still had some control over her tongue, but her eyes were constant traitors. His chuckle was soft, deep.

"If you're through tempting me," he whispered, "we might as well finish lunch."

"I wasn't tempting you," she howled.

"You tempt me every time I see you."

"You must be a sex maniac."

"It's just that I love you very much."

They spoke in whispers, their voices low. Betsy wished he would move away from her; the way he was half leaning on her body, touching her flesh with his, was making her muscles feel like water. She wanted to writhe out from under him, but she could not move a single muscle. Her body was telling her it was so pleasant here—even so ecstatic!—that it would not respond to the commands of her brain.

"How about another sandwich?" she asked weakly.

"Let me feed you."

She glowered up at him, but since she could read the stubbornness in his eyes, she had to admit defeat. "All right, all right. You can feed me."

He rose up off her, pulled her back to a sitting position, and, taking a sandwich, held it to her. She took a bite out of it, chewed.

The humor of the situation touched her then, and she laughed, saying, "You're an idiot."

"Sure I am. I'm crazy about you. Here, take another bite."

She might as well, she thought. He was going to pester her until she did. She bit again, chewed. After a few more bites it seemed only natural.

"Care for a sip of lemonade?"

"You going to feed me that, too?"

"Sure am."

She shook her head but accepted his services. They were sitting side by side, he was right up against her with his arm about her, but she did not move away. There was no sense even trying to get away, she told herself. He would just come after her.

When the sandwich was done, he nodded. "Now you can feed me."

"No way."

"Please?"

His voice was very tender. Betsy sighed, muttering, "Oh, all right."

He bit her finger when she offered him a sandwich, but gently, and his eyes were laughing at her. She could not remain angry at him, he was so much like a little boy. She began to smile back at him and in a minute had entered into the spirit of the moment. She even filled a cup with lemonade and held it so he could drink.

When they were done, they lay back on the blanket to sunbathe a little more. Betsy spent her time thinking about this husband she had. Or to be more specific, her own reactions to him. Why did she almost swoon every time he hugged or kissed her? She had never reacted like that to the other men whom she had dated. Of course, none of them was her husband. Did that make the difference? N-no, she didn't believe so.

She let her thoughts run around in circles and could never quite decide what she ought to do. Stay married with him until the end of her sabbatical, then return home and divorce him? Or go through with the divorce while still in England, so that she would have no ties to sever by the time she went back to the States?

"How about another swim?"

His words cut into her thoughts. She lifted a hand, shading her eyes from the sun, and looked at him. She was remembering what happened between them last time they went swimming.

"You'd better go alone."

"Come on. I won't put a hand on you. Promise."

"Oh, all right."

They waded into the cool water, and it felt good on her hot skin. They swam side by side out into the middle of the river and floated for a time. Betsy had to admit —even if only to herself—that she was enjoying this day,

MY TREASURE, MY LOVE

They drove for him, fists hammering at him. Betsy stared, hardly breathing, her eyes huge and round. They would kill him! She found herself putting a hand on the car door, opening it. Then she raced toward the donkey engine.

Jim was fighting furiously, hammering his fists at the men, one of whom was going down. He was taking blows, too, she saw, reeling back a little, then plunging in against his opponents.

Betsy lifted the edge of a tarpaulin, saw tools stored there. Her hand reached for a big wrench. With the wrench in her hand she turned toward the fighting men.

"I'm coming, Jim," she called.

One of the attackers swung on her, just as she herself was swinging the wrench for his head. The wrench landed, the man fell away, and she turned to watch Jim slugging hard against the lone man who faced him.

He was driving him back and back. The man's face was bloody; one of his eyes was closing; she could make out dark bruises on his face. She stood awed by the fighting fury that possessed this big man of hers. He knew how to use his fists, all right. Betsy felt pride swell up inside her.

Then a hand caught her and yanked her sideways. A hard hand thudded against the side of her face. Betsy reeled back, felt the wrench pulled from her grasp.

"Jim," she screamed. "Watch out."

She fell, landing hard. Dazed, she tried to make it to her feet, seeing the man who had taken the wrench from her leap at Jim.

Jim whirled, an arm up to guard his face. The wrench drove into his arm. Betsy heard the thud it made and winced. Jim leaped, his fist driving at the contorted face of the man with the wrench. His blow landed. The other man staggered back.

But then—

The man whom Jim had been pounding drove in on him, hit him with his body, drove him sideways. The man with the wrench swung it hard. The metal thudded into Jim's head, knocked him backward, off his feet. Even from where she stood Betsy saw the blood on his head.

Lynna Cooper

She screamed and came to her feet to run forward. The man with the wrench lifted it high, drove it down at Jim's head. Betsy hurled herself at him, knocking him sideways. Yet the wrench landed with a sickening sound. Had it broken the skull?

Betsy fastened her teeth in the arm of the man, biting hard. His hand rose, slamming into the side of her head. Betsy felt the world swimming all around her, knew she was falling. . . .

She opened her eyes. She was lying on the ground, and it was dark. For a few moments she did not know where she was. She pushed against the ground, feeling pain run through her. She collapsed and lay there a moment, trying to stifle the panic that held her.

After a moment she tried again and made it to her knees.

She looked around her.

She saw Jim, then, lying still and silent, not far away, and she recalled the blows he had taken with that wrench.

"Jim," she whimpered. "Oh, Jim."

Tears were in her eyes as she crawled toward him.

Chapter Nine

He was dead.

He lay so still, so motionless, that Betsy knew he could not be alive. She crept toward him, sobbing bitterly, angry at her body for being too weak to stand, for not having the strength to let her run toward him.

She came to him at last and, on her hands and knees, stared down into his still, dead face. Sobs racked her body, and she was vaguely aware that she was whispering his name over and over.

There was blood on his head and bruises on his face. There was something wrong with his arm, too.

Trembling, she put a hand to his face, ran her fingertips tenderly over those black-and-blue marks. Her lips were quivering so uncontrollably she could not speak. She was aware only of an agony that was in her very bones.

Her head bowed, she rested it on his chest and began to weep. Her tears flowed; her body shook. Her arms slid up and went around him, as though she could cradle him against all pain, all danger.

"Don't die, Jim," she wept. "Please don't die. If you do, I'll die, too. I just can't live without you. Please, Jim. Please. . . ."

There was no movement at all in his body. She could hear no heartbeat; he lay with his face upturned to the stars, eyelids closed. Betsy stared down at him through the tears flooding her eyes and squeezed herself against him.

Lynna Cooper

The night was cool around her, and faintly she heard the cry of a distant bird, the lapping of waves against the shore. She wept on, her tears staining his shirt, her arms holding him almost convulsively. She burrowed her face against his chest and told herself she wanted to die, too.

"Hey."

It was a mere whisper of sound.

Betsy froze. She could not believe what she had heard or thought she had heard. She lay there, not moving, disbelieving her own ears. Then, very slowly, she raised her head.

His eyes were open. He was looking at her.

She whispered, "Jim? Jim? Are you—are you alive?"

"I think I am. But my head hurts. And my arm."

She got to her knees, staring down at him. "I've got to get you to Dr. Baines. But I can't possibly carry you. Oh, Jim! What can I do?"

His chuckle was faint. "Help me get up. I feel as though I've been broken in half. Here, take my hand."

She helped him rise to a sitting position. But his face was so contorted with pain that her heart seemed almost to stop. Betsy bent, put his arm about her shoulders, then struggled to lift him.

It took a long time, perhaps ten minutes, but she finally got him to his feet, where he stood swaying, breathing harshly. His right arm was about her; the other seemed to hang at an angle.

"Is it broken?" she whispered.

"Afraid so. That was some clout it took. But my head —that hurts worst of all."

"Can you make it to the car?"

"I think so—but slowly."

It took her five minutes, with time out to stop and let him rest, before she got him into the Shelby Cobra. Then she ran around it, slid in behind the wheel, and started the motor.

"Dr. Baines, where does he live?"

"Just beyond the center of town, along the road to Algarkirk."

After that neither spoke. Betsy gave her attention to

MY TREASURE, MY LOVE

the car, to the road ahead, even as another part of her worried over him. She had been so sure he was dead back there. It had seemed, too, that a part of her had died with him as well. But now that he was alive, she was going to do all in her power to keep him alive.

With a screech of brakes and a slide on dirt, she pulled the red car into the little parking lot that was set to one side of Dr. Baines' home and office. Then she ran around the side of the car, opened the door, and told Jim to lean on her.

His legs were wobbly, he staggered, but he took her at her word, leaning his body on hers so that she had to struggle to stay upright. The few feet to the front door of that office seemed to take forever.

The door opened suddenly, and a nurse was standing there, horrified eyes on Jim Manners. Then she was leaping forward, moving to his other side, helping Betsy get him into the office.

"What happened?" the nurse gasped.

"He was attacked by three men," Betsy managed to say. "One of them hit him with a heavy wrench a number of times."

"You come right inside," the nurse ordered.

There were people in the waiting room; they all stared as Betsy and the nurse guided Jim across the room and through a door. The nurse made Jim sit down, and ran to call Dr. Baines.

The doctor came at once, his stethoscope flying. He took one look at Jim, then waved his hand at Betsy. "You wait outside, young lady. I have a lot to do to this fellow."

She went out into the waiting room and sat down, letting her head sink against the backrest. Her eyes closed. She was aware that the other patients were staring at her, that they were dying to question her, but she was in no mood to answer them.

She had too much to think about. What was going to happen now? She would have to stay here and nurse Jim back to health, help him with the arm that must surely be broken. There was no way she was going to leave him now and go away. It was almost as though fate were telling her something.

In time Jim came out, his arm in a cast and sling, his head swathed in bandages. But his step was firm, he walked like his old self, and when his blue eyes saw her, they lighted up. The nurse walked beside him, a hand on his arm, as though to guide him.

She said to Betsy, "He's a very lucky man. His arm is broken, and he has had a concussion; but he'll be as good as ever, with a week or two of rest. He must do nothing strenuous, and the doctor will want to see him in a day or two. The doctor will also make his report of the attack to the authorities."

Betsy nodded, looking up at Jim. "Can you manage by yourself?"

He shook his head. "No, I'd better lean on you a little."

Out of the corners of her eyes she saw the nurse's lips twitch. But she slid under Jim's good arm, told him to lean on her. That good arm caught hold of her, began to squeeze her. Not at all the way a sick man might hold on either. Betsy glanced up at him suspiciously, but his face was bland.

"All right," she murmured. "Let's go."

He walked along beside her without any difficulty, she noted, but he still clung to her with that arm. From time to time he squeezed her even tighter.

"I don't think you're hurt very much," she finally told him just before they came to the car. "That good arm of yours is just as strong as ever."

"Is it too much for you? I just don't want to fall."

Her glance was filled with suspicion, but there was little she could say. He *had* been hurt, after all. And she really didn't have any way of knowing whether he was telling the truth about falling or not. But she had her suspicions.

She drove home slowly, carefully, as though a bump might send lances of pain through him. She would have to take care of him now, making certain that he was comfortable, that he had everything he needed. A tiny thrill of pleasure ran through her, and she admitted to herself that she would enjoy caring for him.

MY TREASURE, MY LOVE

She was braking the car before the house when she remembered dinner. In dismay she turned to him. "What about food?" she asked.

"Not to worry. There's plenty in the freezer. How are you with steaks?"

"Charcoal-grilled?"

He laughed. "Perfect. But you'll have to cut mine for me."

She fussed over him as though he were a sick child, making certain that he was comfortable before she went to raid the freezer. She found a big sirloin that was enough for a small army and lugged it out to the grille on the terrace.

She was lighting the charcoal when he appeared to seat himself and watch what she did with grave eyes. His constant staring bothered her somewhat; it was as though everything she did were being held up to his scrutiny.

When the charcoal was white and giving off plenty of heat, she put the steak on, letting it sear on the outside first, then making certain that it would cook inside.

"Rare?" she asked, eyebrows raised.

"Not too much so," he answered.

She mixed the salad, then put up a small table on which they would eat by candlelight. She lifted the steak, halved it, and plopped down the larger portion on his plate. She began to cut it with a steak knife.

"You're quite domestic, really," he said gently.

"I'm just doing what must be done."

"But so well."

Betsy eyed him. "Sarcasm is not called for."

He looked stricken. "I was only trying to praise you. Must you go around with that chip on your shoulder forever?"

"No. And—I'm sorry."

"A kiss would make me feel a lot better."

"You feel all right."

"No, honestly. Just a little one, to convince me that you don't mind doing all this for me. I feel a big drag, you know, helpless like this."

He didn't look at all helpless, except for that sling

Lynna Cooper

in which his arm rested. He said again, "I don't think I could eat a thing unless I got that kiss."

"Ohhh, all right!"

She leaned over him, put her mouth to his, fully expecting that his good arm would go around her. But it did not; his lips pressed hers, and when she drew away, he did not stop her. She almost resented his not trying to grab her.

They ate in the silence of the early evening, the two candles she had lighted on the table reflecting the brightness off their faces. It was quiet around them; there was only the faint hum of an insect or the cry of a distant bird. Betsy let the quiet seep around her as she sat, drank the coffee she had made, and watched him fuss with his arm sling.

"Does it hurt?" she asked.

"A little. Not too much. But I'm happy to note that you're asking."

"Oh, Jim. Why must you say things like that?"

He put out his good hand toward her. With a sigh, she let him hold her hand. At least, if she kept that hand busy, he wouldn't be putting it on her or wrapping her up in his good arm.

A thought touched her mind. She couldn't let him sleep in that sleeping bag! He would have to be in a bed, tonight and for several nights to come. Well, she herself could use the sleeping bag.

But when she mentioned it, he shook his head. "No. No sleeping bag for you. You'll use the bed, too. With me."

Betsy straightened up and yanked her hand free. "I will not. You can have the bed, of course. That goes without saying. But I will not sleep in it with you."

"We are married folks, you know," he reminded her gently.

"Legally, perhaps. Not—not in any other way."

"That isn't my fault."

She leaped to her feet. "I'd better clear the table."

His hand caught her wrist. "Oh, sit down. Why do you always shy away from me when I remind you that I'm your husband? Are you so afraid of me?"

MY TREASURE, MY LOVE

"N-no. Not really."

She wished he wouldn't look at her in that way, with all that tenderness showing in his eyes. He made her feel like a heel. An unfeeling heel, at that. That tiny smile was on his lips again and made her wonder what other idea he would throw at her.

"You'll have to undress me, too," he murmured.

"Never!"

Jim sighed. "I'll have to sleep in my clothes then."

She scowled at him. Were all husbands this difficult? She recalled that her mother had told her that all men were little boys, especially when they were hurt or injured. They carried on as though they were racked with agony; they needed fussing over and attention; they made a great many demands.

Even her father was like that, her big father who was almost as strong as Jim. She recalled the time he had sprained an ankle and had hobbled about, looking very abused by life. Of course, he had been at the digs, had suffered heat and wretched living conditions, and one would think that he would be used to something like a sprained ankle. Her mother had fussed over him, made certain that he was comfortable, had fed him cool lemonades and baked his favorite pie.

She giggled at the memory.

It was Jim's turn to scowl. "What's so funny?"

"Do you have a favorite pie?" she asked, the merriment showing in her eyes.

Suspicious, he asked warily, "And if I do?"

"I thought I'd bake it for you tomorrow if you did."

He got a pleased, silly expression on his face. "Can you really bake?"

"I'm not exactly helpless," she snapped.

His look was thoughtful. "I haven't had a chocolate cream pie in I don't know when."

"Chocolate cream it is then. And now how about another cup of coffee? Are you comfortable like that? Would you like a pillow behind your head? And maybe one under your bad arm?"

The silly look on his face made her want to bite him. But she rose and got two pillows, propping his arm on

Lynna Cooper

one and his head on the other. Then she heated the coffee and poured him another cup. As she moved about, she was conscious of his eyes following her.

"You know, you're really a born wife," he told her. "I just can't understand why no other man has ever grabbed you."

"They've tried."

"And you resisted them. Good. I'm proud of you. You waited until I came along."

Betsy wanted to bop him. Instead, she only smiled and patted his head, then ran her fingers through his mop of blond hair. "Are you comfortable? You're sure? Is the coffee all right? Hot enough?"

"Why aren't you like this more often?" he asked plaintively.

Her fingers wanted to grab his hair and pull. But she beamed at him and said softly, "You never gave me the chance. You were always so independent, so rugged."

"Remind me to break my arm every so often. It's worth it, to see you acting human."

She eyed him. "Will you be all right here while I do the clearing up?"

"I'll miss you."

She snorted and walked away with the dirty dishes.

When she was done, she came back and joined him, and they sat on the terrace as the day darkened into night around them. It was quiet here, very peaceful. In the stillness they could hear the faint sounds of the cars moving along the road, but they seemed far away.

Twice Jim yawned, and it came to Betsy that he might be hinting. She knew he could not undress himself; she guessed she would have to help him. But he'd better not try any funny stuff. He would have to sleep in the bed, naturally; she could not ask him to sleep in the bag. And she would be beside him.

Of course, she could make up a bed in another room and sleep there. But she felt that if he should need her in the night, she really ought to be on hand to fetch his medicine. Could a man with a broken arm be amorous? Betsy wasn't sure, and she didn't trust him. Not one iota. Still, she could fend him off.

MY TREASURE, MY LOVE

"Time for bed?" she asked.

"It might not be a bad idea. I am a little tired."

"Can you make it upstairs?"

"If I could lean on you just a little."

"Your legs aren't broken, are they?"

"No, but I'm still very weak."

He looked about as weak as a man-eating tiger. But she remembered her mother with her father, so she came to him, aided him to his feet, and let him put his good arm around her. He squeezed her more than was necessary, but she bit down on her tongue and remained silent.

When they got to the bedroom, she turned on the lights and pulled down the covers. Jim stood in the middle of the room, making no move to assist himself. Betsy sighed and walked to him, began unbuttoning his shirt.

"Stop staring at me," she muttered.

"I can't help it. You're beautiful."

"Pooh."

"There's a little lock of hair that keeps bouncing against your cheek when you move. It seems to be telling me that your cheek is the smoothest, softest cheek in all the world."

"Will you move so I can slide down your shirt?"

"You're not listening."

"You're talking nonsense."

"Did I ever tell you your lips are—"

"Jim!"

She got his shirt off, scowling as she did so. She would never admit it, but his voice was soothing her, his words were getting to her. Did he really think her cheeks were so smooth and soft? That her lips were, well, whatever he had been going to say about them?

"On the bed," she ordered. "I have to get your pants off."

She knelt to lift off his shoes and peel down his socks. Then she unbuckled his belt and helped him slide down his trousers. Her eyes went over his body for a brief moment. He was big, all right, and covered with muscles. No wonder he could squeeze her so hard!

"All right. Into bed," she ordered.

"No pajamas?" he asked, his eyes dancing.

"Can you put them on by yourself?"
"Of course not. You'll have to help."
"Then no pajamas."
"You're a hard woman, Betsy. Absolutely without pity."
"Oh, get into bed and cover yourself up."
He did what she asked and slid over to the far side. Then he said, "You will join me, won't you?"
"Yes, yes. Just as soon as I bathe and get into my own pajamas."
"I'll wait," he said.
She marched into the bedroom, took a shower, and dried off. She slid into her pajamas which hid her very effectively, she felt.
As she was about to slide under the covers, she stared hard at him. "You stay on your own side, you hear?"
"Of course, darling."
Darling. Ha! She turned off the light.
Betsy heard him moving and tensed. But he was only settling himself. She let her eyes close, but she remained awake. At least for a little while. But soon tiredness got the better of her, and she slept.
Once she woke in the middle of the night to find that he was nestled close to her. A little too close, she told herself. She wriggled away, turned the other way, and fell asleep again.
In the morning sunlight, she woke to find that she herself was cuddled against his big body. Apparently she had turned in her sleep and, finding him big and warm beside her, had gravitated toward him.
His good arm was around her.
"Good morning," he said softly.
She wriggled to free herself, but it was no use. "Let me go," she muttered.
"In a little while. Let's just talk, as a husband and wife ought to do in the privacy of the marriage bed."
"Now look, James Manners!"
"Am I so disturbing to you? Does the mere touch of my body make you want to forget your maidenly virtue and hurl yourself at me and cover me with kisses?"
She was aghast. She stuttered, trying to get out a denial.

MY TREASURE, MY LOVE

He leaned over her and kissed her. Very gently, but right on her mouth. She did not fight him—she didn't want to hurt his broken arm, she told herself—but he did not pursue his kiss. He lay back and stared at the ceiling.

"I can see our life stretching out before us," he went on softly. "There'll be a lot of mornings like this, when we cuddle together." That arm of his was like an iron bar, keeping her there, half on top of him. "And I suppose that we'll make love, too, when you just can't restrain yourself any longer. But that will be all right. I'll always be in the mood."

"You're insufferable!"

"I think I'd like ham and eggs for breakfast, darling."

"I can't cook if you keep holding me here."

His arm squeezed her even closer, and she was certain that he could feel her body. She could feel his, all right. And the touch of it made her senses swim. If he didn't release her pretty soon, she was not going to be accountable for what might happen.

Then his arm went away, and she was free. Just for an instant she did not move. But that was her body betraying her again, she knew. It wanted to remain here beside this man who was her husband. It wanted to have that arm back around her again. And it also wanted—here she scowled a denial—his mouth to come down on hers again in a kiss.

She moved away swiftly then. She snatched up her clothes and scampered into the bathroom to change. Jim was still in bed, watching her as she came out.

"Don't forget me," he said with a grin. "I'm going to have to be dressed by you."

She tossed her pajamas to one side. "All right. Might as well get it over with. You can't eat breakfast in your shorts."

She was frying bacon when the front doorbell rang. Jim, who had been watching every move she made, rose to his feet. "I'll answer it. You go on."

She could hear voices then and tensed when she recognized one of them as belonging to Glenna Forrest. She turned from the stove to stare at the doorway. How could

Lynna Cooper

that woman have the nerve to come here after what happened to Jim yesterday? Betsy was positive that those men who had attacked Jim had been hired by Glenna to work the drill and the donkey engine.

The voices were coming closer. She turned back to the stove, lifting the bacon from the frying pan.

"—won't take no for an answer, Jim. You can have the best of everything. Servants to wait on you, a good doctor to check your arm. You can have a good rest."

Betsy swung around. What was this?

Jim came into the kitchen first, his face bland. Right behind him came Glenna Forrest, looking like a model out of *Vogue* in a Jamaica blue cotton A-line dress with a big white bow at the top. She appeared cool and lovely. Betsy felt out of place in her slacks and blouse.

Jim said, "Glenna wants us to move over to her place, says it'll be a lot easier to take care of me there."

Betsy felt the tears come into her eyes. She blinked, turned back to the frying bacon. It took a moment or two before she could master her feelings.

She knew now that all those things he had said to her yesterday had been only so many words. Obviously he felt that he would be better off under Glenna's care. Ha! Maybe *she* would undress him then.

"Whatever you want," she muttered.

She would not look at him; she broke some eggs into the pan and watched them sizzle. Betsy told herself to get hold of her emotions. It might be better for Jim Manners to go to the house that Glenna Forrest called home. She was obviously wealthy; Jim would be waited on hand and foot. There would be good doctors available, maybe even specialists.

She could hear them talking behind her, but she kept her attention focused on the eggs. Still, a tiny voice began to whisper in her ear. Didn't Jim suspect Glenna Forrest of instigating those three men who had used that drill and donkey engine yesterday?

Was she also responsible for that attack on him?

She wanted to whirl around and scream out her suspicions, but she told herself that Jim Manners was a man

MY TREASURE, MY LOVE

of the world. If he suspected Glenna Forrest, he would be able to deal with her.

After scooping up the eggs, she placed them on two plates, added bacon.

She turned and placed a plate before Jim and put the other where she would sit. She poured coffee for them both, then sat down.

"We have a very fine cook at the castle," Glenna was saying.

"Betsy is no slouch with a skillet."

"I didn't mean to imply that. But she has so much to do, taking care of you. It isn't fair to burden her, Jimmy."

"It's no burden," Betsy found herself saying. "He's my husband, and I'm perfectly able to attend to his needs."

"Of course you are." Glenna smiled coldly. "But at the castle we can do all these things even better."

"It's up to Jim," Betsy muttered.

"Then it's all settled. You can pack and drive over—Jimmy knows the way. He ought to; he's been there so much in the past. I'll wait."

Betsy noted that Jim was eating by himself, and quite capably, too. Last night he had made her feed him. If Glenna had not shown up, would he have asked her to feed him again? She told herself that she missed his dependency on her.

It would be worse at that place Glenna Forrest called the castle. There would be a battery of servants, she guessed, all running around and waiting on him. He'd love that, naturally. Her eyes slid sideways at him.

He seemed happy enough. Much too happy, as a matter of fact. The prospect of staying at this castle of which Glenna spoke must appeal to him. It did *not* appeal to her. It was on the tip of her tongue to refuse to go, but Jim looked at her suddenly—almost as though he were reading her mind—and gave her a headshake.

Ha! If he thought she was going to go there and be pushed off somewhere while he and Glenna had a rare old time for themselves, he had another think coming. Still, it wouldn't harm her to play along, if only to see what Glenna's home looked like.

Lynna Cooper

She did the dishes while Glenna took Jim and wandered off.

After that she went upstairs and packed her bags. She would take everything with her that she had brought to England. It wasn't all that much, she reflected with a wry twist to her lips. When she had packed for her trip, she had gone overboard and bought new clothes—a cocktail dress by Helen Rose, two pairs of new slacks (which weren't all that new any longer), a Kugler cardigan with some fancy pocket embroidery, several dresses, and some blouses—but she had the knowledge that her clothes would appear poor indeed beside those of Glenna Forrest. The A-line she was wearing today must have set her back a lot.

Betsy sighed. Oh, well. There wasn't anything she could do about it. She had her wardrobe with her and was stuck with it. Her chin lifted. What difference did her clothes make anyhow? Glenna Forrest was on her home grounds; she would have all sorts of fancy garments to wear, to attract Jim's eyes.

She carried her bags downstairs. As she did, she remembered Jim's broken arm. She would have to pack for him, too; he couldn't manage it with only the one hand.

Betsy trudged upstairs and began to open drawers.

She found a big, much-battered suitcase and started to fill it with what shirts and underthings of his she could find. While she was occupied with this, Jim walked in and closed the door behind him.

When she gave him a side glance, he said slowly, "I know how you must feel, but please, just play along with me."

She straightened slowly. "Play along? So you can have yourself a ball with that one?"

"You don't understand. And I can't tell you."

"No need to make a mystery out of it. That woman can give you all the luxury and attention you need. I understand that. In a way, I don't blame you at all. It must be quite dull, just having me around for company."

He came across the room with two long strides and stood staring down at her, anger smoldering in his eyes. "It isn't that at all. Will you forget your female vanity for just a little while?"

MY TREASURE, MY LOVE

Betsy gasped. "Female vanity? Now you listen here, Jim Manners! I—"

"I want to give that woman her comeuppance. Can you get that through your pretty head?"

"But—"

"Just listen to me. There's nothing between Glenna Forrest and me. Never has been. Oh, I've taken her out to dinner a few times over the years since I've been coming to visit Jason, but that's all there is between us."

"She acts as if—"

"I know she does. It's her way. Her father is one of the richest men in England, and Glenna has never been able to forget it. She's always gotten everything she's ever wanted. Except me, I guess."

"Well, now she's going to get you."

His good arm came out and around her, bringing her up against him, almost crushing her. It was disturbing to Betsy to be this close to him, just as his blue eyes told her it was as disturbing to him.

"She is not going to get me. You have me. Can you understand that? You're my wife. Mrs. Jim Manners. If I can't have you, I don't want anybody. You hear me?"

Very meekly she murmured, "I hear you."

He looked down at her suspiciously. "You mean it?"

She nodded. She did not believe a word he said, but why should she have an argument with him? She would play the part of dumb wife, go along quietly, and then at the first chance she had, she would run away.

Oh, yes. This mockery of a marriage had been doomed from the beginning; she had kept it up only because she was too lazy to take the one big step to get away from him. She would do anything he asked; she would efface herself at that castle; she would bide her time.

His arm slowly eased its pressure. She pulled away from him, turned to his open bag. "Do I have everything you'll need? There are a couple of suits and slacks in the closet, I haven't put those in yet. But is there anything else?"

"No, no. You've been wonderful."

She went to the closet, began to pack the rest of his clothes. He stood and watched her, frowning a moment.

"Are you taking everything from here? All our clothes?"

"Don't you think it's best? We'll probably need all we have, if life at the castle is going to be as exciting and as social as I imagine it will be."

"You may be right."

But he said it dubiously, as though he might be suspicious of her. When she went to lift the bag off the bed, he brushed her aside. "Let me carry it, it'll be too heavy for you."

She trailed after him as he left the room.

Glenna Forrest was waiting outside, face raised to the sun, eyes closed. She turned when she heard their steps and gave Jim a big smile.

"You ride with me, Jim. Your wife can follow in your car with the luggage."

Without so much as a glance at Betsy, Glenna took Jim by his good arm and walked him to the Silver Cloud. Betsy stood and watched Jim climb in. She felt like a sore thumb, standing there with the bags on the ground waiting to be stored in the Shelby Cobra.

Well, she knew where she stood all right. But then she had known all along, hadn't she? She opened the trunk of the red car, lifted and put the bags in, then slammed the top shut. She moved to get behind the wheel.

The Silver Cloud started off. Betsy followed it, not wanting to lose sight of it. If she should lose it, she hadn't the slightest idea where to go.

Fortunately Glenna Forrest seemed in no hurry. Probably talking a mile a minute with Jim, she thought darkly. Make hay while the sun was shining. So let her; she herself certainly didn't have any hold on him.

After a time, though, her spirits lifted. Maybe it would be a good idea if Glenna got Jim into her clutches, made him realize that she could give him everything that Betsy couldn't. Then he would let her get the divorce; she could take her little trip around England to see the sights and then head for home.

Somehow that idea didn't cheer her too much.

They drove for almost an hour, until they came in sight of a huge stone building set amid a veritable sea of closely cropped grass. Betsy gave one look at it and

MY TREASURE, MY LOVE

felt her spirits wilt. Was this where Glenna Forrest lived? It was a real castle all right.

Her eyes, when they left the road, could see battlements and turrets, sheer walls in which tiny openings could be seen—they were arrow slits, she knew, where archers had sent their shafts out upon besiegers—and tall windows set into the stone walls. There had been a moat here once; there was a deep ditch all around the big building where water had once been and which was now filled with flowers.

How rich could the Forrests be?

Betsy drove over a roadway above the ditch and into what had once been a huge courtyard. She braked and stared around her at some staircases, at glass windows, at oaken doors. She saw Glenna get out and move around her car to assist Jim.

Ha! He didn't need her help. It was only his arm that was broken, not the rest of him. Then they walked off together, Glenna clinging to him, talking up at him, her laughter ringing out. Apparently they had both forgotten about her.

Betsy opened the car trunk, lifted out the bags. She scowled down at them. She was going to have to carry them, it seemed.

She lifted two of the bags and staggered after the others. Not until she was mounting the stone staircase up which they had gone did the door open and a uniformed servant come hurrying down to meet her, reaching for the bags. Betsy handed them over with a sigh of relief.

She trailed after the butler through a hallway, the walls of which were dark, polished wood, and came into a big room which she assumed must be a living room. There was a huge fireplace, and the stone walls were thick with antlers hung on them. Crossed swords and other ancient weapons occupied what space was left by the antlers.

She moved toward the front windows, which were gigantic, and looked out over a vast expanse of lawn. It was very pleasant here; in other circumstances she might have enjoyed this visit to an English castle. But at the moment Betsy felt abandoned, somewhat forlorn.

Lynna Cooper

Where was Jim? What had Glenna done with him?

She was commiserating with herself when a step sounded on the stone flooring. A big man stood looking at her quizzically. He was tall, his hair was white, and his face was ruddy, as though long exposed to the elements. His dark eyes studied her, then began to twinkle.

"You'll be his wife," he said softly.

When Betsy looked surprised, he chuckled. "Mrs. Jim Manners, I mean. Am I right?"

She nodded, and he advanced, his big hand stretched out in greeting.

"I'm Archibald Forrest. I'm Glenna's father. Though"—and here his eyes laughed at her—"I'm not responsible for her actions. Haven't been for a long time. I take it she's after your husband."

Betsy closed her mouth. She hadn't met such frankness in years. She nodded, though, and managed a smile. "She is. And she doesn't pull any punches either."

"That's Glenna." His gaze sharpened. "She's out to get him, you know. With all guns firing. If you want to hold him, you'd better go scooting after them."

"No." Betsy shook her head. "No, if she wants him, she can have him. I'm tired of this mock marriage of ours."

"Mock marriage?"

She turned away and looked out the window. Against her will, tears came into her eyes. "It was a mistake, our getting married. I knew it right from the beginning. We don't love each other; we only did it to please an old man who is now dead."

Archibald Forrest moved up to stand beside her. After a brief glance at her face he also stared out the window. Then he said quietly, "My dear girl, I don't believe a word of it. You love that man, and if I were you, I wouldn't let my daughter get him off by herself. She'll ruin your life if you do."

"I—I don't c-care."

He chuckled gently. "Liar. You're head over heels in love with him. I'm a great judge of character. You listen to me now. You go after them and stay with them. Other-

MY TREASURE, MY LOVE

wise, my daughter will get him away from you. I've seen her operate in the past. And she wants your husband very much."

A coldness seeped down inside Betsy, making her shiver.

Chapter Ten

For three days Betsy endured it. She was put in a little bedroom while Jim was given a big, sprawling room that was located next to Glenna's bedroom. No matter how early she rose, Jim and Glenna were always up before her and had left the castle so that she ate a lonesome breakfast. She wandered like the proverbial lost soul along the passageways of the castle—occasionally she would meet Archibald Forrest hurrying here and there—and she would take long walks out across the vast green lawns and between the trees of the little forest that was part of the property.

At dinner she would see Jim and Glenna, always with their heads close together as they chatted and talked. Once or twice he would look at her and smile or nod his head approvingly. Approving what? she asked herself disconsolately. Her conduct in letting Jim have Glenna all to himself? She was just somebody who was in the way here. Nobody talked to her or paid her any attention, except Glenna's father. And he was too concerned about the affairs of his castle to bother his head over her.

One morning, when she woke, she made up her mind. She was going to leave this place. She would pack her bag and take the Shelby Cobra and drive back to Fosdyke. She would pick up the Hillman and leave the red car for Jim to find when he returned to the house. She would then drive around England, have her little vacation, and take a plane back to the States.

Lynna Cooper

Angrily she brushed away the tears that came into her eyes. She was a little ninny, weeping like this. It was what she wanted, wasn't it? Of course. Her freedom meant all the world to her. She would divorce Jim, then be free again.

She dressed in slacks and a blouse, she packed her bag—let Jim pack his own, she snarled under her breath—and then trotted downstairs to eat her lonely breakfast.

She gorged on sausages and eggs, drank three cups of coffee and smoked a couple of cigarettes, dwelling on the fun she would have, tootling off by herself. She would stop anywhere she wanted; she had all the rest of the summer. She would be answerable to no one but herself.

For some strange reason this did not cheer her.

When the castle was quiet, she rose and crept upstairs. She got her luggage, then tiptoed down the staircase and along the hall. She opened the oak door, peered out. There was no one in sight. Hurriedly she fled down the stone staircase and ran to the red car.

It took her only a moment to toss her bags inside, then slide behind the wheel. In moments she was moving over the little stone bridge and along the road that would take her to the highway.

Betsy drove through a landscape that was blurry from the tears in her eyes. From time to time she would rub the tears from her lashes with an angry hand, telling herself over and over that she was an idiot. That was what she wanted, wasn't it? Her freedom? Of course it was. Well, she was doing something about getting that freedom, so why was she crying?

"I'm a nut," she muttered.

Twice she took the wrong turn but righted herself after traveling across an unfamiliar countryside. The day was glorious with sunshine, but she paid little heed to it, being too sunk in misery to care about anything except that misery.

She stopped at a tiny inn just outside Quadring to eat lunch. The food was tasteless—at least to her—but she forced herself to eat. As she munched without enjoyment, she told herself that she must get used to the idea of being by herself again.

MY TREASURE, MY LOVE

She had to put Jim out of her head, out of her heart. Her heart? Now why should she think of her heart? She didn't love the guy, and the heart was the traditional seat of love. She did *not* love Jim Manners.

Oh, no? Then why all the gloom?

She pushed what remained of her sandwich around the plate. She missed him, yes. She admitted that. But anyone would miss a companion with whom one had shared the adventures of the past few weeks. It took a little time to get used to being by herself. That was all.

Betsy sipped her coffee and smoked a cigarette.

She drove the rest of the way in a pall of gloom. She could not shake that feeling, no matter how she talked to herself. Always that hidden voice was there, somewhere inside her, chiding her.

Well, what was I supposed to do, just mope around by myself while Glenna and Jim had themselves a time?

She had her pride. And her pride would not let her stay around that castle.

She came into Fosdyke as the shadows were lengthening and made her way toward the house. It was dark, unlighted, and it did not seem at all friendly as she parked the Shelby Cobra and made her way toward it. She would stay the night, and in the morning she would slide into the Hillman and drive north toward Lincoln.

She moved into the front hall, then threw open a couple of windows to let in the fresh air. She cooked a couple of chops which she took from the freezer, and made a meal of them.

Carrying her bag, she went upstairs.

She was half undressed when she heard the sound.

It was not a loud sound, just a brief creak, as though a foot had stepped on a loose floorboard. Betsy paused, turned toward the open door of the bedroom. She tiptoed out into the hall. She was opening her mouth to call out—her heart was beating wildly at the thought that Jim had missed her and had come to be with her—when she heard a board creak again.

She drew back into the shadows.

Who was downstairs? Not Jim, certainly! He would

have bellowed out a greeting; he would have been racing up the stairs to scold her.

Betsy moved into her room, slid the blouse back on, and tucked it inside the slacks. Her heart hammered wildly. Who were these housebreakers? Some local youths here to steal? Or—

No. They would not be locals. Local boys would be talking, calling out to one another. These men moved as silently as shadows, with just a board creaking to betray them every so often.

Were they those three men who had attacked Jim?

Oh, no. Not those three! They would show her no mercy if they found her. And they would find her if they searched the house, as they seemed to be doing. Betsy turned and stared around her wildly. Where was there to hide?

The bathroom. Of course. It had a lock.

She scampered to it, closed the door behind her and snapped the lock. Then she sat on the edge of the tub, hands clasped between her knees, just listening.

Very faintly she could hear them now. They must have decided that the place was empty, for it seemed that she could hear their voices. And footsteps, yes. They were searching the house.

But for what? There was silverware downstairs, heavy plate here and there. Any sneak thieves would latch onto that and then make a getaway. But these men seemed to be still searching. They were coming upstairs now; she could hear them talking.

Betsy shrank back. Would they try the bathroom door and find it locked? If they did, they would know she was in here. Would they break down the door? If they did, what would happen to her?

She could not breathe suddenly. And her heart was pounding so heavily she was sure they would hear it. Her eyes watched the doorknob.

It turned; the door moved slightly as though someone were tugging at it. Then she heard a voice crying out, "It's locked from the inside. There's someone in there."

There was a flurry of whispers which she could not understand. Then something hurtled against the door.

MY TREASURE, MY LOVE

Again it slammed into it. Betsy knew that the door would yield; it had never been built to withstand several men hurling themselves at it.

"Wait, wait," she called out.

Her trembling fingers touched the lock, moved it. Then she opened the door.

Three men stood there, crowded together. These were the same three men who had fought Jim, hard and grim-faced men whose eyes stared at her coldly. Betsy shivered. There was no pity, no mercy, in any of them.

"Wha-what do you wa-want?" she asked.

"Jason Tilden's maps, his papers. Where are they?"

She shook her head. "I don't know. He was very secretive."

Two of the men looked at the third, a big man with a hard, flat face. He was clad in dirty clothes, and there was a rough look to him. His face was in need of a shave, but his brown eyes were clear and merciless.

"Take her downstairs into the cellar. Tie her up and leave her," he growled.

Betsy eyed him in horror. "Nobody will come here! I'll die."

The big man shrugged. "If you remember where Tilden's maps are, I'll see to it that someone comes to turn you loose. Otherwise. . . ."

Betsy licked her lips. What did she care whether they had the maps Jason Tilden had drawn? Her life was more important than those maps.

"He had some maps downstairs in the library. I saw them. He kept them in a flat drawer under the bookcases."

"Show us."

On trembling legs she edged past them, went out into the hall. They came after her, apparently to prevent her from trying to escape. Betsy knew she had no chance to run away. She could never elude them, reach the Hillman before they would be upon her.

She walked into the library, stared around it in something like horror. Books were everywhere, they had been yanked down and thrown aside after they had been searched. The flat drawers, too, had been ransacked. She stared at the drawer in which Jason Tilden had kept his maps. It was empty.

"In there," she whispered. "He kept the maps in there."

"There are no maps there."

Her heart was a leaden ball. What had happened to the maps? Had Glenna Forrest stolen them? She turned and stared at the three men.

"They were there. I saw him take them out, then put them back."

The men looked at her, and then the flat-faced man said, "Take her downstairs. Tie her up so she can't wriggle free. Then we'll get on with the search."

The other two men pushed her ahead of them, down the cellar stairs. A single light bulb burned down here, and there was a musty smell everywhere. She could make out the stone walls, a few wooden planks put together to form tiny rooms. A hand was at her shoulder, pushing her into one of the rooms.

Someone brought cord and tied her hands together behind her back. A hand shoved her, making her fall hard on the stone floor. Then other hands were tying her ankles together, knotting them.

A man brought out a handkerchief, pushed it into her mouth, then used cord to tie it in place. When they were done, the two men stood and stared down at her, coldly and without pity.

Betsy tried to beg, to ask them to loosen her bonds, but she could make only muffled sounds. Her eyes were big as she looked up at them, and tears were already forming in them. The men glanced at each other, then turned and left her. An instant later the light went out.

She lay in darkness, bound so tightly that the cord impeded the flow of her blood. Terror was alive in her. She would die here in this deserted house. There was no one to come for her; no one knew where she had gone. Oh, she had been most careful about that. She had crept out of the Forrest castle as might a thief. No one had seen her leave. Jim would not be alarmed at her absence until the evening meal, when she would not appear at the dinner table.

He would know then that she had left, taking his red

MY TREASURE, MY LOVE

car. But would he know where she had gone? He might guess. Yes, he might guess all right. But he would assume she had left him, was going off somewhere to be by herself. He would have no way of knowing she was in any danger.

Betsy wept.

For a time she listened to their footfalls sounding in the house, hoping that one of those men would come down here before leaving and loosen her bonds or even set her free. But then she heard the front door slamming, and after that there was no sound, none at all, in the house.

Betsy struggled, wriggling across the stone floor, bumping into some tools that clattered down around her, slamming into the wall. It was hard to see down here; it was as black as moonless midnight. And it was getting cold. She began shivering steadily.

She tried to loosen her bonds, but they were too tight; the men who had put these cords on her had made certain that she would not be able to pull a wrist loose. Yet she worked on, sobbing fitfully, fighting against the despair and the sheer horror that held her.

After a long time she slept.

She came out of that sleep, heart pounding. Had that been a sound which had awakened her? She lay there, scarcely breathing, straining her every nerve, her every sense.

Yes! That was a footfall on the floor above her.

Betsy moaned against the handkerchief that gagged her. It was Jim! He had become alarmed at her absence; he had borrowed a car and come here. He had seen the Shelby Cobra, her Hillman, and he knew that she was somewhere in the house.

But—

Why didn't he shout out her name, calling her?

For whoever was in the house was being as secretive as those three men had been when they had come here searching.

Betsy's eyes were wide as she stared into the darkness. Should she try to let the person up above know that she was down here? The wooden wall was close by; all she need do was roll toward it and then hammer with her shoes against it. In the utter silence of the house whoever was up there would hear her.

Then she heard the cellar door open. A beam of light shot past the doorway of the little cubicle where she was tied. Then she heard a foot descend on the top step of the cellar stairs.

Betsy hardly breathed. Who was it? *Who?*

The steps continued down the stairs, sounded on stone now. Eyes big, Betsy watched that moving beam of light. Had one of those men been sent back to—kill her?

Then the light was moving inside the little room where she lay on the floor. Its radiance touched her, ran over her, from her bound feet to her face, dirty and tear-stained. Betsy made a whimpering sound. She could not see the person behind that flashlight. Not clearly anyhow. Yet it seemed like a thin man. Or—a woman.

"Well, well. So this is how it ends for you."

The voice was that of Glenna Forrest.

Betsy closed her eyes. She could expect no help, no sympathy from that one. She would hardly be so heartless as to leave her here to die. Would she? Inside her, a voice told her that this woman would indeed be that heartless.

"Out of my life, out of Jim's," the voice went on. Betsy sensed the cruelty in it, the sheer jealousy.

The light turned and moved away. Betsy wanted to scream out not to leave her here, not down here in the dark. But the feet moved away very firmly, very assuredly. And that light beam went with them.

Glenna Forrest mounted the stairs, closed the cellar door.

Then she went away.

Betsy wanted to scream. She did scream, she guessed; at least she was making sounds in her throat and mouth that the handkerchief smothered and muted. She wriggled and twisted, trying desperately to free a hand, even a leg. Her tongue tried to work the handkerchief out of her mouth, but whoever had done the tying had been too adept at the job.

She subsided in tears.

MY TREASURE, MY LOVE

Betsy sobbed, moaning. There was nothing she could do. She would die down here, and—she supposed—someone who came to look at the house years from now would find her skeleton. She slept then. It was a disturbed sleep; she dreamed of strange beings that came into this cellar where she lay tied and that reached out clawlike hands for her. In her dream she screamed and screamed, yet there was no one to hear her. Whimpering, she woke and sobbed on.

Again she slept, exhausted, but this time she did not dream.

And then—

There was a sound, very faint. Yet it was enough to reach down inside her sleeping mind, to wake her. Her eyes snapped open; she stared at blackness. Had something waked her? She did not know. Desperately her eyes went around in the darkness, seeing nothing.

She heard it now more clearly. It was a footstep on the floor above. It paused, as though waiting. She heard a voice calling, faintly.

"Betsy! Betsy, are you here?"

That was Jim's voice, and her heart leaped. She tried to call out to him, but the handkerchief in her mouth muted the sound. Her eyes ran wildly around in the utter darkness. Was there any way to let him know she was down here?

Betsy remembered the wall and began to roll about in the hope of finding it. When she thudded into it, she worked her body about until she could lift her bound legs and hammer her shoes against the wooden barrier.

The sounds she made reverberated throughout the cellar. But were they loud enough that Jim would hear them? She banged her shoes again and again on the wall.

A door opened somewhere above her.

"Betsy? Are you down there?"

She could not reply. The handkerchief choked her too much. But she could slam her shoes against the wooden partition, and she did.

She saw the beam of a flashlight then and nearly wept with relief. Again her shoes hammered at the wall, and it seemed that she heard Jim cry out almost in echo.

157

Lynna Cooper

Feet thundered down the stairs; she saw the flashlight beam grow larger.

Once more she hit the wall, banging it.

Then Jim was standing in the doorway of the little room, his light directed down at her. She heard his muffled curse, and he was leaping forward, putting down the flashlight to gather her up in his good arm and hold her.

"Oh, my God," he was whispering over and over.

His hand went to the cord that held the handkerchief in her mouth. It was falling away and he was removing the wadded handkerchief from her mouth.

"Are you all right? Are you?"

She tried to speak but could not. Her mouth was too dry. It was hard even to swallow. "Jim," she whimpered. "Oh, Jim. . . . ."

"There, there. I'll have you free in a second."

He turned her, worked at the knots that held her wrists, her ankles. When they fell away, she could not move so he had to help her to her feet with his good arm and hold her. She was trembling, shaking uncontrollably. The tears came, too, flooding from her eyes as she clung to him.

"Oh, Jim, it was awful. So . . . awful! They tied me up and—and left me here to—to die. That woman came—Glenna Forrest—and stood over me and to-told me that when a-anyone found me, I would be a—a skeleton."

He said nothing, but his arm tightened about her.

It came to Betsy that Jim might resent this, that if he were so much in love with Glenna Forrest, he might not want it known that she had abandoned Betsy. She must be careful, she told herself. She did not want Jim knocking her out and tying her up again and leaving her.

"Here, walk around. It'll restore your circulation. I'll hold you. Come on now."

He was extraordinarily gentle with her, she thought, as he turned her and, with an arm about her, made her walk up and down. It hurt her so much at first that she almost fell. But his arm was supporting her, gripping her firmly. And after a time she found she could move without pain.

Jim bent and picked up his Everready, then, with his arm about her, guided her across the floor and to the

MY TREASURE, MY LOVE

stairs. "Take it easy," he murmured. "Anytime you want to rest, just tell me."

She made it without stopping, though when they came to the top of the stairs, she leaned against him and shook a little. The lights were on, she saw, and it came to her that she must look like the wrath of God. Her clothes were all over dirt; there must be smudges on her face.

Her eyes went to Jim, and she saw his blue eyes filled with love and tenderness. "I must be a fright," she whispered. "I'm so dirty!"

His eyes smiled at her. "Upstairs, then, and into a hot tub. It will relax you." He hesitated, then murmured, "I'll bet you haven't eaten either."

"Oh, yes. I ate. But—but I would like a bath. What time is it?"

He glanced down at his Longines-Wittnauer. "Almost five in the morning."

"Five?"

He nodded, smiling grimly. "You were in that cellar a long time. I didn't know where you were, but—"

"Go on, Jim."

He glanced away from her. "I knew you'd run off, of course. I guess I didn't blame you for that. So I packed my own things and told Archibald Forrest I was going after you. That was when I learned that Glenna had left the house.

"I didn't expect her to harm you, but knowing Glenna, I couldn't be sure. So I came here just as fast as I could. Of course, I had to borrow a car to do it, you'd taken the Cobra. I managed to drive with my good arm—then I got a flat. By the time I'd had it fixed it was pretty late. I came on and found you."

"It was those same three men who fought you at the dig who found me here, tied me up, and left me."

He nodded grimly. "I guessed as much. But never mind that now. Upstairs you go, get into that tub, and relax. Then you're going to get a good sleep."

She obeyed him, letting him guide her up the staircase, still with his arm about her. He left her sitting on the bed while he went into the bathroom to run the hot water and fill the tub. She began undoing the buttons of her blouse.

He came back to stand before her, smiling down at her. "I'll leave you now, but I'll be within call, if you should need me. And sleep as long as you want. You've had a bad experience. I want you to put it out of your mind, forget it."

She nodded dumbly. She was so exhausted she felt she would agree to anything. Of course, she would never forget what had happened, but maybe a good night's sleep would help ease it out of her mind.

He went out and closed the door.

Betsy undressed, slid into the tub, and rested. Jim was on guard; nothing could happen to her now. It was all she wanted to know.

After donning her pajamas, she crept into bed and slept.

When she next opened her eyes, it was either late morning or early afternoon, she wasn't sure. She slid out of bed and dressed, staring into the mirror at her face. Her experience last night didn't seem to have affected her any, or maybe it was because she had been able to sleep so long and so soundly.

Hurriedly she slid into a shift dress by Pipard, combed her thick black hair, and tied a scarf around her head. Then she ran downstairs.

Jim was just coming in the front door. He paused and stared at her, and something about the way he looked at her sent a wave of pleasure all through her. He came across the hall floor to stand before her.

"You're beautiful," he whispered.

"Oh, I'm not," she protested, but she could not deny the delight she felt.

"Come along and have lunch. I'll get it ready."

"I can do it."

"Looking like that? As if you'd just stepped out of a bandbox? No way. You just sit down and be gorgeous."

She smiled up at him. He took her arm and brought her into the kitchen, plopped her down in a chair. He moved to the stove, lifted out a pan.

"It's almost two, so I figure a combination breakfast and lunch ought to keep you until we hit London."

Betsy gaped. "London?"

"That's where we're going. For a vacation of sorts. We've

MY TREASURE, MY LOVE

had enough of this place. Besides, those three men know about it and . . . they might come back."

A coldness came into her body. With Jim here beside her, she had almost forgotten about those men and Glenna Forrest. But they were not likely to forget her. If they knew she was no longer tied up in the cellar, they might be back to finish the job. Betsy shuddered.

Jim put a cheese omelet before her, with buttered toast and coffee. Betsy had not believed she was hungry, but she finished it all.

"You drive your Hillman back to the rental agency. I'll follow you in the Cobra. I've already phoned and made reservations at the Grosvenor House on Park Lane."

"Oh."

She thought about that, of sharing a room with Jim in a big London hotel. Anything was better than remaining here, of course. If it had been up to her alone, she would already have fled. But to share a hotel room with this husband of hers who was no true husband . . . she would have to give that some thought.

His lips were grinning at her. "They have twin beds, you know."

She had to laugh. It was as if he were reading her mind.

"Besides," he added, "if I'm with you all the time, nobody's going to be able so much as to lay a finger on you."

There was that, she admitted and felt somewhat better.

"Your clothes," he told her when she was crushing out her cigarette. "Are you all packed?"

She nodded. She had pulled out her pajamas last night and this outfit she was wearing now. Otherwise, all her things were neatly in place in her bags.

"Time to get moving then," he announced.

Jim took the lead in the red Shelby Cobra, with Betsy trailing after him in the Hillman. He drove slowly, because of his bad arm, so that she was able to keep up. Through Spalding and March they went, south toward Cambridge.

It was a long drive for England, more than ninety miles. But the traffic was not too heavy, and they made good time. Once in London, they drove to the car rental place, where Betsy turned over the Hillman.

Lynna Cooper

She was lifting out her wallet when Jim pushed her aside, lifting bills from his own wallet. "This is on me," he told her.

Betsy waited until they were walking toward the Cobra before she began arguing. "I shouldn't have let you pay, Jim. I hired the car. It was my responsibility."

"Will you come down off your high horse? I'm your husband. If you run up any bills, I pay for them."

"But you shouldn't. I can stand on my own two feet."

"Sure you can. You're the independent type. I know that. But indulge me. I've never had a wife before, and I find it's fun, paying her bills."

She glanced up at him. "You must be wealthy to adopt that offhand attitude."

"I have a few dollars. I've never spent very much on my jobs; all my lodgings and food bills were taken care of by my employers. I've banked a lot of my salaries and commissions."

"You sound wealthy."

He grinned. "I'm not poor. Now will you please stop worrying about my finances and enjoy yourself? One of the first things we have to do is buy you some clothes."

"What's the matter with my clothes?"

"Absolutely nothing. Only you need some new things."

"What for?" she asked suspiciously.

"To go out to nightclubs, to have dinner at some fancy restaurants I know. You don't want to appear dowdy, do you?"

"Dowdy!"

He laughed as he opened the car door. "Just a figure of speech. You'd never be dowdy no matter what you wore. Now stop arguing. Get in and start enjoying this."

He drove easily through the London traffic to Park Lane. Grosvenor House was a huge place, she saw as she walked into it. The lobby was immense, part of it was partitioned off by glass walls, and there was an air of comfortable luxury about it.

Only when she was going up beside Jim in the elevator did she begin to get misgivings. She would be alone with Jim here; there would be no one on whom to call for help

MY TREASURE, MY LOVE

in case he became . . . well, amorous. She glanced sideways at him.

He looked like the proverbial cat that had swallowed the canary, she thought morosely.

Chapter Eleven

They walked into a room fitted with two rather large twin beds, a writing desk and chair, and two comfortable chairs. Underfoot was a thick carpet, and a cool wind was blowing in through the open windows.

Jim tipped the porter who had carried their bags. The porter went out and closed the door behind him.

"Want to freshen up?" Jim asked. "We'll eat here tonight, then get a good night's sleep. Tomorrow we want to be up early. There are a lot of places to see, and we want to hit them all."

Excitement stirred in her. She was basically a country girl, and the idea of being in a city like London was pleasant. She moved to the dressing table and studied her reflection. Her cheeks were heightened with color, and her hair, though somewhat windblown, was not quite as disheveled as she had thought. She began tucking stray wisps into place.

She turned to find Jim watching her, smiling faintly.

"What is it?" she asked.

"Can't a man admire his wife?"

"Oh, Jim. Don't be silly."

Why was her heart thumping so loudly? Just because they were off by themselves in this London hotel room didn't make any difference in their lives. Oh, they were married all right. But they weren't in love.

He came up behind her and gripped her shoulders. She stared at the mirror, seeing his face reflected there. Was

Lynna Cooper

that adoration in those blue eyes? And tenderness? Betsy could not drag her gaze away from his. She felt the nearness of his body, the strange excitement welling up inside her.

"I th-think I'm ready," she whispered.

"You'll be the most beautiful woman in the room."

"I'm not beautiful," she heard herself mutter.

"You're crazy. You're the most glamorous woman I've ever seen. I've always known you would be like this. Now come on, stop tempting me and let's go eat."

His hand had to push her before she could move. What was the matter with her? She had been almost hypnotized by his eyes, standing there. If he had turned her around just then, to kiss her—well! She would have kissed him back, all right. She knew that, even though she despised herself for the knowledge.

What was going to happen between them when they came back here after dinner?

Betsy shivered, but it was a pleasant shivering.

Get hold of yourself, you idiot! He'll be able to see right through you; he'll know that all he need do is grab hold of you and you'll melt.

No. No, I won't!

Liar! Liar! Liar!

Then they were in the dining room, and the maître d' was leading them toward a table lighted by a candle, off somewhere in a darkened corner. It was intimate, that corner; they were almost hidden from the rest of the diners by heavy curtains. The maître d' held her chair as she seated herself.

Then Jim was ordering drinks and smiling at her.

"Now isn't this cozy? Just the two of us, no treasure to fuss over, nothing to do but enjoy ourselves."

Betsy nodded. How could she tell him she was on pins and needles, being so alone with him, wondering what was going to happen when they were upstairs in that big bedroom? It wasn't at all like being back there in Fosdyke. Here they were strangers to everyone; there was no one to help her if she should call out.

For help? Against her own husband?

Betsy, you're loopy!

MY TREASURE, MY LOVE

The drinks were delicious, pleasantly cold. They lingered over them before Jim reached for the menu and asked her what she wanted to do tomorrow.

"Anywhere you want to go, anything you want to do." He smiled.

Betsy shifted uncomfortably. What did she want to do? Anything at all, she decided morosely. Just so that Jim was with her.

Now what made her think that? Was she growing so accustomed to having him at her side that if they were parted, she would miss him that much? It must be.

He was talking again. "I thought the Tate Gallery right after breakfast. And possibly a shopping spree in the afternoon. How does that sound?"

It sounded like a bit of heaven. Betsy nodded, her eyes fixed on his, vaguely aware that she was flushing as a result of seeing the adoration in his own eyes.

"It'll be wonderful," she murmured.

His smile was gentle. "It will be. I'll see to it."

He was ordering then, smoked salmon as an appetizer, jugged hare with red currant jelly for himself and lamb kidneys madeira for Betsy. She watched him, discovering that he was quite adept at handling a menu, just as he was at about everything else he tackled. It came to her that this husband of hers was quite a man of the world.

They did not talk much as they ate, and for once, Betsy was quite happy about it. The food was delicious, served in elegant style. The thought came to her that if she went on living with Jim Manners, she might very well put on weight.

"It will never do," she muttered almost to herself.

"How's that again?"

She flushed, laughing. "I was telling myself that if we go on living together, I'll add pounds and pounds. I'm not used to stuffing myself on such meals."

"Nor am I. Out on a job, I'm lucky to find a sandwich to nibble on. But when I get within reach of a fine restaurant, I do like to indulge."

For dessert they settled on soufflé Grand Marnier.

When they were finished with their coffee, Jim suggested

Lynna Cooper

a walk. "Help to settle some of the food. Besides, it's a little too early to hit the sack just yet."

They strolled along Mount Street to Berkeley Square and circled it, walking leisurely. The night was calm, with little or no wind, and overhead Betsy could make out a star or two. Betsy would have walked on forever, postponing their return to the hotel and that room, but she discovered that her body was betraying her. Again and again she had to stifle a yawn.

Jim said slowly, "We'd better be heading back."

"No. There's no need for that. It's so pleasant, just walking."

Laughter struggled in his throat with the words he spoke. "Personally, I think you're all but sleepwalking right now."

"I'm fine, Jim. Really I am," she protested.

"But you'll be even finer back at the hotel."

He turned her firmly and held her arm in his as they moved along. There was no arguing with him, she knew. Once he made up his mind to something, that was it. So she trotted along beside him, wondering just how she was going to get out of her clothes, with him there in the bedroom.

She needn't have worried. He went up with her to their room, pushed her inside, and told her he was going downstairs to buy some cigarettes. Gratefully Betsy slid into the bedroom and ran for her pajamas.

She was asleep when he returned.

The next morning she woke to the smell of food. Lazily she turned over, then sat upright. There was a tray in the room, covered with napkins, and Jim was sitting on a chair, smiling at her.

"Come on, lazybones. I'm waiting breakfast on you."

Betsy cast longing eyes at her robe, which was on the back of a chair across the room. Why hadn't she thrown it over her bed last night? She scowled, sighed, and threw back the covers.

As she ran for the chair, she felt his eyes on her. These pajamas were much too thin, almost transparent. Flushing, turning her back, she slid one arm into the robe, then the other, and belted it, giving him her back.

"Selfish," he whispered, laughter in his voice.

MY TREASURE, MY LOVE

She let her eyes slide toward him. She had to admit he was acting the proper gentleman. He wasn't trying to grab her and kiss her—as she had fully expected him to do—nor was he even suggesting that he leave his bed and climb into hers. Fat lot of good that would do him! Still, she had to admit that he was behaving quite correctly.

They ate breakfast together, planning their day.

They found a taxi and drove to the Tate Gallery. Betsy was surprised at his knowledge of the great painters represented there; he talked on about their lives, the quality of their work, until she found herself staring up at him in wonder.

"How come you know so much about all this?"

His eyes twinkled as he said, "I came here with Glenna once."

Betsy scowled.

But her momentary annoyance did not last. He was too charming, too considerate of her feelings for that. He was gentleness and thoughtfulness personified. He insisted she rest from time to time (almost as though she were an invalid), and he sat beside her, telling her about the books he read while on his jobs.

"I don't get too much time for reading, but I manage," he confided. "I suppose if I had a wife along on those trips, I wouldn't have any time to read."

"Why not?" she asked suspiciously.

"A loving wife needs attention. She doesn't want anything to keep her husband's thoughts from her."

"There are other things in life besides love."

"But nothing as exhilarating."

"Nonsense," she snapped.

He leaned closer. "You don't mean that."

With him so close, she really didn't know what she meant. She fumbled with her handbag, not daring to look at him because she knew very well what he would read in her eyes. She jumped to her feet.

"Let's go look at some more pictures."

They lunched at Fortnum and Mason's, and then Jim insisted that they shop for clothes for her. Despite her protests, he bundled her into a taxi and told the driver to take them to Selfridge's in Oxford Street.

"An evening gown," Jim suggested. "For dancing. You do dance, don't you?"

She nodded, not trusting herself to speak. If they danced —which they hadn't done yet, she realized—he would take her in his arms. And she wouldn't guarantee her behavior when he did that. She just couldn't. Her body was betraying her enough as it was.

He selected something in black velvet, cut low in front and in back. Betsy stared at it, horrified. It would show so much of her!

"I just couldn't," she murmured.

"Of course you can. Try it on."

When she sneaked a look at the price tag, she came close to fainting. All she had to do was show him how much it cost, and he would tell her to take it off.

Yet when she had put it on and stared at herself in the mirror, she felt royal. The black velvet enhanced her skin, matched her thick ebony hair. She was really quite lovely in it, she told herself. But it cost far too much.

Jim stared when she came out of the dressing room. His eyes went over her, and they seemed to glow. He did the walking, moving around her, studying her. "Exquisite," he muttered. "We'll take it."

"Do you know how much it costs?" she whispered.

He shrugged, and Betsy eyed him carefully.

"You do need a wife," she muttered. "At least you need somebody to watch your wallet."

The evening gown was only the first of his purchases. He took her from department to department, buying her underwear—frothy, frilly stuff that was utterly transparent, which she wouldn't be caught dead in—and dresses, stockings, shoes. She watched with a frown as he wrote out a check.

As they left Selfridge's, she said, "You'll be a pauper if you keep on like this. Don't you have any idea of the value of money?"

"My father always told me a wife was an expense. I'm beginning to see how right he was."

She stuttered indignantly, only to be caught in his good arm and squeezed. His laughter rang out, causing heads to turn.

MY TREASURE, MY LOVE

"You're impossible," she muttered.

For the next three days they went everywhere in London, or so it seemed. At night they went out to dine, to dance. During the days they visited the London Museum, the Kensington Museum, the National Gallery, Westminster Abbey, and the Houses of Parliament.

It was a constant coming and going, and Betsy felt that she had been swept up into a maelstrom of movement. She went here and there; she feasted as never before; she wore clothes that enhanced her loveliness.

She went with Jim when he visited a doctor to look at his arm. She watched as the cast was removed and the bandage was changed, listened as the doctor told him the arm would be as good as new in a few more days, that it was knitting nicely.

Sometimes she protested against the pace he was setting; she told him a man with a broken arm ought not to be doing so much. He would listen to her politely, then explain that going about London with her helped him forget the arm.

For a week they acted like vacationers.

Then, one morning, Jim told Betsy that he had to go away for a couple of days.

She eyed him suspiciously. Why was he leaving her? To run back to Glenna? No, that couldn't be it. At least she didn't think so.

"I'll leave you plenty of money," he assured her. "You'll stay here, of course, but you can have yourself a time, waiting for me. There must be dozens of places you'll want to visit, places we haven't seen."

"Why?" she asked. "Why are you going away? And where?"

He smiled but shook his head. "My secret, darling. And it has to remain so. But you'll be all right here. Nothing will bother you."

His words put a chill in her. She pushed a bit of food about on her plate, staring down at it. She really had no rights, no rights that a real wife would have, for instance. She had to accept what he told her, she guessed.

But the worry was still inside her as she stood on the sidewalk and watched him drive off in the Shelby Cobra.

Lynna Cooper

Was he going to Glenna? Or back to the dig? If it was anything else, she felt certain that he would tell her, confide in her.

All that day she wandered the streets of London, visiting the Old Curiosity Shop, taking in a movie in the afternoon, eating at a lonely table at night. She bought a paperback to take upstairs with her, to read in bed.

But when she had changed into her pajamas and was curled up in bed, she found the paperback was not enough to hold her interest. She put it down and stared across the room. What was the matter with her? In the past she had always enjoyed reading, snug in her bed. But now, for some reason, it seemed tasteless.

Where was Jim? What was he doing?

How could he have left her here all by herself?

"Ha!" she exclaimed. "No wonder he left you, you big ninny. What fun are you, holding him at arm's length all the time, afraid he might grab you and toss you onto a bed?"

For a moment she was appalled at herself. "What am I saying?"

She sat upright. A wild elation was running all through her veins, a sense of discovery that sent chills of delight up and down her spine. "You big goose," she whispered. "You simple ninny! You love the guy!"

No. It could not be. She was her own woman.

"Are you?" she sneered. "He's been gone one day and you miss him like crazy! You wish he were here, in the next bed."

Not in the next bed. In her own bed!

She did, she did! She knew it now, when—when it was too late. How long was a guy going to put up with her ridiculous notions, when there were plenty of girls around, all of them very willing to take hold of Jim Manners and get him to love them?

"I have to find him, tell him," she whispered.

Well, she was too late for that. He had gone off believing that she was one cold fish. And she didn't blame him. Tears welled up into her eyes.

"I'll be different, Jim. I will. Just come back to me."

Why? Why should he come back to the likes of her? If

MY TREASURE, MY LOVE

she were Jim, would she come back to somebody who acted as if he had the hives? Or poison ivy? She would not. She would know when enough was enough.

She wept then, turning over and burying her face in the pillow. "Jim, Jim! Forget how I've been acting. Come back to me. Come back. . . ."

She fell asleep like that, with her tears staining the pillowcase.

In the morning she made up her mind. She was going after him. Oh, yes, she was. And when she saw him, she was going to throw herself into his arms and beg him to forgive her. She had been a silly, stupid girl. But now she finally realized that he was the one man for her in all the world.

Ah, but would he listen to her?

Suppose he were with Glenna Forrest? Suppose he had had enough of her indifference and had gone off to find a woman who was willing to accept him as a lover, as a . . . husband? He would divorce her and—

"No," she whimpered. "No! I won't let him."

So what are you going to do about it, Betsy Jane?

"I'm going after him! Today. Right now."

She dressed in a tweed suit, one of those Jim had bought her. She wore the frilly underwear under it, too. And the stockings he had bought her, and the shoes. Even the pocketbook she snatched up was a gift from him.

She ate a good breakfast, telling herself she was not going to stop for lunch, not until she had found her husband.

Ah, but where was he?

She had no way of knowing.

She would drive to Fosdyke, of course, and begin her search there. It was possible that Jim had been thinking about the digs, about somewhere else to shift his drill and donkey engine. He might well be there, yes. If he were not there, she would drive to the Tilden house.

Maybe he was there with Glenna.

Her heart turned over inside her at that thought. If he really had run off to be with Glenna, then there was no use in her living. She might as well die. And she could blame no one but herself for her predicament.

She had been a silly little fool. She hadn't known love

173

when it practically jumped up and bit her. No, she had to be standoffish; she had to deny all her instincts, even her very body that had been perfectly willing to be in love with Jim Manners a long time ago.

Determinedly, she made herself finish her breakfast, sip the coffee. She needed food in her; she wanted to be at her best when she came up to Jim. She wouldn't hesitate; she would just run up to him, throw herself into his arms, and tell him over and over (until he got sick of hearing it) that she loved him more than life itself.

First of all, she would have to hire a car. Well, that was no problem. She caught a taxi, drove to the same car rental agency she had used before. She saw the same Hillman, thought it a lucky omen, and pointed it out as the car she wanted to rent.

By midmorning she was out of London, driving north.

The day was clear, with intermittent splashes of sunlight and cloudiness. It was cool; she drove with the windows half up. When it rained as she was going through Ely, she watched the windshield wipers swing back and forth and smiled. Each of those wipers was like the beating of her heart, measuring off the miles.

Through March and Guyhirne she drove, and now the rain was behind her and the sun was warmly comforting. She lowered the windows and let the cool breezes flow past her. They seemed to cheer her, as though all the world were trying to whisper to her that she was doing the right thing.

When she came to the turnoff road, she hesitated. Could Jim be at the digs, making one last try for the treasure? She wouldn't put it past him. On impulse she swung to the right, took the narrow dirt road that wound toward The Wash. If Jim were there, she would join him at work.

No matter if she were wearing a good tweed suit. What difference did it make if she got it dirty, so long as she was beside the man she loved?

She swung about the last turn, and The Wash lay before her.

Her foot hit the brake, and her heart sank. There was no sight of the donkey engine. It was gone, as was the drill. The land lay barren. It looked as desolate as she felt.

MY TREASURE, MY LOVE

Could she be wrong? Had Jim gone off to the castle where Glenna Forrest lived? Was he even now with her, holding her and kissing her, there in her home? She swallowed, tears coming into her eyes.

No, Jim. No! Please God, let me be wrong!

She sat gripping the wheel for long minutes, staring straight ahead. She could not be wrong. Jim wasn't like that. He couldn't be, not after those days they had spent in London walking hand in hand, enthusing over a picture or a statue, sitting side by side in the theaters they had attended, or dancing so close together at the nightclubs.

"I—I hope he isn't anyhow," she whimpered.

Well, it was all her own fault. She had no one else to blame. If her frigidity had turned him off, turned him away from her, she really couldn't blame him. Only herself. Her hands held tight to the steering wheel.

"Jim, I've got to find you," she whispered brokenly. "I have to tell you what a simpleton I've been. Please! Please wait for me, wherever you are!"

The Tilden house? Was that where he was?

Ah, but why would he go there? Unless—unless, of course, he was with Glenna Forrest and they were making love in the bedroom which she and Jim had shared . . . without love.

She had to see, to learn the truth.

She backed the car, turned it, sped along the dirt road. Her foot trod hard on the accelerator. Once the car skidded at a turn, and she was forced to slow down. But not by much. Now she was on the regular road, and here she could make good time.

Betsy drove along the drive toward the Tilden house, eyes busily scanning the drive. There were no cars here, none at all. Perhaps they were in the back of the house, where the garage stood. But when she swung around there, everything seemed locked up, abandoned.

She got out of the car. They could have driven off for groceries, of course. If they had, there would be some indication that they were here. Glenna's clothes, for instance, or Jim's.

On wobbly legs she made her way to the front door,

Lynna Cooper

fumbling in her purse for the key she had retained. She slid the key into the lock, opened the door.

The house was very quiet. It seemed stuffy, too, as though it had been long closed up. She went up the staircase and into the big bedroom which she and Jim had shared.

The bed was made up, neatly. There were no clothes in the closets or in the drawers. Betsy stood a moment, nibbling at her lower lip. They weren't here then. She had taken this ride for nothing.

She went down the stairs, glancing around her. Into the kitchen she moved and saw that it was as she had left it. Her eyes swung sideways toward the cellar door. The door was closed.

She remembered her terror down there, tied and gagged. A shudder ran down her spine. Never in her life had she been so terrified. She remembered her father telling her that if something frightened her, to do it over and over again, until she lost her fear.

Betsy smiled faintly. "I ought to go down and take a peek in that place where they left me. I'll bet it will seem quite harmless to me now."

On impulse she snatched up the flashlight from where Jim had left it the night he had rescued her. She snapped it on, then swung about, opened the cellar door, and put her foot on the top step.

Her heart thundered. Fear held her motionless.

"Now what am I so afraid of?" she muttered angrily. "There's no one here; there's nothing down there to harm me. Get moving, Betsy Jane."

She walked down the staircase, the flashlight held firmly in her right hand. All she need do was take a peek in that cubicle where she had been a prisoner; then she could turn around and run if she wanted.

She advanced toward the opening. Her flashlight beam lifted, focused on the cubicle. She walked forward a few steps, standing in the opening, and ran her flashlight beam around the interior.

And then she began to scream.

176

Chapter Twelve

There was a body in there, tied as she had been tied!

Her nerveless fingers dropped the flashlight. She stood shaking, unable to move a muscle. Her mouth made little, whimpering sounds, and it seemed that her legs were made of sponge. She sagged sideways until the upright held her.

"No," she whispered. "No. It ca-can't be."

But she had seen the body, seen it with her own two eyes. There was no mistake. Betsy bent, and her hands fumbled for the flashlight. If that person were alive, she would free her, just as Jim had set her free.

She could do no less.

Once again her light played over the figure. She saw its immobility, its . . . deadness.

Up above a door slammed, and she heard voices.

Betsy whirled and fled back into the darkness of the cellar. She retreated until her back was against the stone wall. Then she flicked off her flashlight.

Who was upstairs? Who? Those three men who had caught her and tied her up, leaving her to die? If they found her here, they would tie her up as they had tied the other woman, the one in the cubicle now. And no one would ever find her. Not Jim certainly. He would have no idea of where it was she had gone.

He would think she had run away from him!

Betsy whimpered. Then she bit her lower lip, hearing feet walking across the kitchen floor. A voice muttered something. Then the cellar light was switched on.

Lynna Cooper

She shrank back into the shadows, hoping that no one would see her in this dark corner. Her eyes went to the staircase and she saw a pair of women's legs in silk nylon stockings. Those legs came down the stairs. Behind them came a man.

Jim!

Glenna Forrest and Jim!

She could see them now all right. They were together, as she had suspected. Her heart turned over inside her, and she leaned back against the stonework, eyes closed, misery flooding through her.

He had gone to Glenna, as she had suspected. She had given him the love she herself had refused him. But—but why were they here in the cellar? Had Glenna killed another woman?

Her eyes snapped open.

Glenna was saying, "I don't know why you want to come down here, Jim."

"I've been trying to find Betsy. And I haven't been able to."

Betsy stared. What in the world was he saying? He knew where she was—or should be: back at Grosvenor House. She opened her mouth to protest, but something within her cautioned her to remain quiet, unseen, and unheard. She watched, eyes brilliant.

They were in front of the cubicle. Jim was pausing, turning to stare inside. And Glenna Forrest was watching him, eyes hard.

"Oh, my God," Jim whispered. "It's Betsy!"

Betsy stared, dumbfounded. What was the matter with him? He knew very well it wasn't she who was in that cubicle! He himself had rescued her. Then why—

"Of course, it's Betsy," Glenna was saying coldly. "She must have pushed her nose in where it wasn't wanted, and that's what happened to her."

Jim swung around, face hard. "You don't seem surprised."

Her only answer was a careless shrug.

"As a matter of fact," Jim went on, "I wouldn't be at all surprised if you knew she was in here—dead."

"Look, Jim. Let's not have any heroics. Your wife is

MY TREASURE, MY LOVE

dead. You and I can get married; we can have a good life together."

Jim was silent a moment. Then he said—and Betsy thought she had never heard his voice so cold, so filled with repressed fury—"I'm beginning to think you killed her, Glenna. Or arranged to have her killed. Is that it? Those three men who attacked me. Were they working for you?"

"Oh, Jim, must you? All this is over and done with. Your wife is dead, but you and I are alive. Come on, we'll just leave that body there until—"

"You heartless bitch!"

The words came out of him like blows against her face. Glenna Forrest backed away from him, a hand up. "Jim, don't force me to—"

Her words trailed off, but Jim pursued them.

"Force you to what? Put my body in there alongside Betsy's? To keep me from shouting out my suspicions to the police?"

Glenna called, "Down here! Down here!"

There was a rush of feet along the kitchen floor above. The feet came racing down the cellar stairs. Betsy saw the three men, the same three men who had overcome her and tied her up, leaving her here in the cellar. Each of the men had a length of pipe in his hand. They rushed for Jim.

Betsy screamed and ran forward.

At the same instant Jim put a whistle in his mouth and blew it.

Betsy dived into Glenna, upsetting her, driving her between Jim and the three oncoming men. Her hand was balled into a fist, which she drove at that face she hated.

She heard Jim yell, "Betsy!"

Then she and Glenna were clawing at each other, turning over and over. Betsy tucked her face against Glenna Forrest even as her fists pummeled her. She was so angry, so furious, that she heard nothing but her fists thudding into the woman, was aware of nothing but Glenna Forrest and her hatred of her.

Hands clutched her, but she fought them off, sobbing

Lynna Cooper

and half-crazy with the fury in her. The hands came back, caught her, lifted her. Arms went around her, holding her.

"Let me go, let me go," she sobbed. "She saw me here and left me to die. She—"

"You're a little wildcat. I never realized you had it in you."

That was Jim's voice, half-laughing, half-awed. She turned in the arm that gripped her, saw that it was Jim holding her.

She sank back against him, whispering, "Jim, darling. I'm so sorry for the way I've acted. Do you hate me?"

His eyes laughed down at her. "This really isn't the time or place, honey."

Something about his words warned her. She turned—still in his arms—and saw half a dozen uniformed policemen and a couple of others who must have been detectives. Off to one side the three men who had attacked Jim were standing, arms behind their backs, handcuffs on their wrists.

Glenna Forrest was there, too, looking rather bedraggled, her clothes torn, one eye swelling darkly, her lips puffy. Her eyes looked hate back at Betsy.

One of the detectives was smiling faintly as he looked at Betsy.

"Are you the person who was tied up in this cellar and left to die?" he was asking.

Betsy nodded. "I am. Those three men tied me up, and left me. That one"—and here she looked hard at Glenna Forrest—"found me and left me here. If it hadn't been for my—my husband, I'd be d-dead by now."

A thought struck her, and she whirled to stare up at Jim. "But there's someone in there now. I saw her. So did you."

"It's only a dummy." He grinned.

"A dummy?"

"Sure. I—er—borrowed your clothes and brought them down here and arranged it. I wanted to confront Glenna with your dead body, so to speak."

The detective said to Betsy, "I assume you'll prefer charges, Mrs. Manners."

Betsy glanced at Glenna, then at Jim. "I certainly will.

MY TREASURE, MY LOVE

And so will my husband. Those men attacked him viciously. They broke his arm. You can check with Dr. Baines about that. They should be punished."

The detective nodded approvingly. "Will you come down to the local police station and sign a complaint?"

"We both will," Jim said.

They stood with his arm about her as the others filed up the stairs and out of the house. She was very conscious of his nearness, of his masculinity. And she loved it. She did! There was nowhere else in all this world that she wanted to be right now but in his arms.

"Your broken arm," she murmured. "Does it hurt?"

"Not a bit. It's mending nicely."

She looked up at him, eyes twinkling. "You might hug me a little tighter then."

His face registered the astonishment he felt. "You're not joking?" he asked.

She shook her head. "Not in the slightest. You've married yourself a wife, Jim Manners, a wife who intends to be very loving, very devoted."

"You feel all right?" he asked.

She put her arms about his neck and drew his lips down to her own. "I'll show you how all right I feel!"

When she let him go, he was breathing hard, and she giggled.

"Hadn't we better be getting over to that police station and sign whatever it is they want us to sign?"

"Yes, but—"

"Come along then."

She took his arm and walked to the staircase. She ran up it ahead of him, then led the way to the Shelby Cobra. She took the keys from him and sat behind the wheel.

"You're driving?" he asked.

"I am. We can make better time this way. Besides, I don't trust my husband to drive safely with a broken arm."

"Hey, now. I told you it was much better."

"You can prove that . . . later."

He eyed her wonderingly as she swung out of the drive. For a few moments he eyed the road ahead; then he glanced at her.

"You're different," he said then.

Lynna Cooper

"I've been a stupid fool. I wouldn't blame you if you hated me, Jim. What must you have thought of me? Here I was in love with you—ever since I saw you that first time, I think—and I've acted like an idiot."

"You love me?"

She glanced at him. "Of course I do!"

"Women," he murmured and sank back against the seat.

They were at the police station long enough to dictate their statements and sign them, Betsy hovering close to Jim as though she were afraid he might vanish into thin air. She made him sit down—to rest himself, she told him—and she made certain that the coffee the police brought him was hot and properly sweetened.

He kept eyeing her like a man in a daze.

Only when they were outside the police station and walking toward the Shelby Cobra did he come out of his seeming paralysis. His hand held her elbow, he looked down at her, and he frowned.

"Let me get this straight," he said then. "You love me? You're accepting me as your husband—in every sense of the word?"

"You'd better believe it."

"I wish I could."

"You just wait, Jim Manners."

She helped him into the car, then drove it away, toward The Wash.

Almost plaintively he asked, "Where are we going? Or is that some sort of secret?"

"We're going to have dinner at that place that looks out over The Wash. I find I'm hungry, and I want you to have all your energy."

Jim hesitated, then murmured, "I guess I'm hungry enough to eat. But afterward? After we have that meal? Do you intend driving back to London in the dark?"

"We are not going back to London. Not until tomorrow, that is. We will spend the night at Jason's house. We own it, don't we?"

"Well, yes. But we don't have any clothes with us, other than what we have on."

"Does that disturb you so much?"

182

MY TREASURE, MY LOVE

He eyed her warily. "I don't have my sleeping bag either."

"Phooey."

They dined on clams, oysters, and beef Wellington, and topped off the meal with wedges of banana meringue pie and coffee. Jim ate under Betsy's watchful eye; she kept asking him if he wanted anything else; she made certain that he left nothing on his plate.

"I'm stuffed," he said at last.

"Good," she said. "We'll take a little stroll around the grounds, just to settle our food."

When he reached for his wallet, she forestalled him. "This is on me, darling," she explained. "It's my way of saying thank you for being so patient."

Her eyes glinted laughter as she added, "I have other ways of showing my gratitude too, but not here."

They walked out along the pathways that overlooked The Wash. It was a pleasant evening; there was a hint of coming autumn in the air that was crisply invigorating. When they came to a railing, they leaned against it, looking up at the moon.

"Jim, what happened to the donkey engine, the drill?" Betsy asked suddenly, turning to look up at him.

"I sold it a few days ago."

She showed her surprise, then asked, "But why? Have you abandoned your attempts to find the treasure?"

He chuckled. "Sure have. Just as soon as Jason died. I went to see his lawyer, you know. That's how I knew you and I had inherited everything. And the lawyer told me, when I mentioned the treasure of King John, that it was useless to try for it."

"Useless? But we found those three gold coins."

"And by rights, by law, they belong to the Crown."

"What?" she yelped.

"Fact. It was King John's treasure; it would revert to whoever sat on the throne of England. Even if we had found it, we would have been forced to turn it over, though I believe we would have received a reward commensurate with the amount of the recovery."

Betsy stared at him. "Did Jason know that?"

"He did. His lawyer told him, same as he told me."

Lynna Cooper

"Then why go to all the trouble we did?"

Jim sighed and stared out over The Wash. "Jason Tilden was a stubborn man. What he wanted, well, he went after." His eyes came back to look down at her. "Like us. He wanted us to marry; it was a dream of his. He'd had it for years. But I guess he just couldn't up and tell us to get married without having some sort of inducement to make us. To make you, actually. I was all for it."

She leaned against him, sighing. "Was I such a little beast? No. Don't answer that. I will. I *was* a little beast. I don't know how you could have put up with me."

"I loved you," he murmured. "Still do, as far as that goes."

She looked up at him. "I loved you, too, though I didn't know it. Can you forgive me, darling?"

"Well, now. That all depends."

She saw his smiling lips and smiled in response. "On what?"

"On whether or not you mean all those wonderful things you've been hinting to me ever since this afternoon."

"You'll see," she whispered.

His good arm hugged her, and Betsy gloried in it. She turned and lifted her mouth to his, was kissed and held so strongly that she could hardly breathe. Yet it was worth a little suffocation, she told herself. This was where she belonged, in his arms. Well, one arm for the nonce.

She turned, and they walked back to the Shelby Cobra. Happiness was like a radiance inside her; it made her positively glow. To think that she could have had all this long ago made her somewhat pensive.

She could make up for it, of course. As she thought this, she turned and smiled at Jim. "How do you feel? Strong? Healthy?"

Jim laughed. "You know, you almost frighten me."

"Never that," she bubbled.

When they were in the car and moving along the road toward the Tilden house, Betsy said, "One last thing, before we forget about everything but ourselves. Those maps Jason had. Those three men looked for them. I did, too, when I thought it might make them let me go. Where are they?"

MY TREASURE, MY LOVE

"I gave them to the lawyer. He's going to send them on to the Queen. If she wants to hunt for that treasure, she has my blessing. Me, I have my treasure."

"Oh? What treasure is that?"

"Don't be dense, darling. It's you."

Betsy glowed some more. Her foot stepped harder on the accelerator. What was she wasting time for, driving around Lincolnshire like this, when she could be home in bed with this husband of hers? She drove deftly, surely, and when she finally braked the car before the house, she leaned back and sighed.

"I'm so happy," she whispered, turning to him. "I never knew such happiness as this could be."

"Well, I'm happy, too, but I could be even happier."

Betsy laughed. "So you feel that way, too, do you? Then what are we sitting here for? Let's get out of the car and into that bed."

They ran across the grass and into the house.

Appendix

Treasure trove is where gold or silver coins, plate or bullion, are found hidden in the earth or any other secret place, and in England, it belongs to the Crown by prerogative right, except when the person who buried it is known, in which case it belongs to him, always assuming he had a valid title to it.

Should the treasure be scattered in the sea or upon the surface of the earth, or lost, or abandoned, then it belongs to the first finder. Any person finding treasure trove must report it to the coroner. Concealment is punishable by fine and imprisonment.

To obtain a franchise to dig for lost treasure, one must apply to the Crown.

Residents of the United Kingdom may hold gold coins without restriction. They may buy or sell coins minted before 1837, but not after that date. They would not be allowed to hold bullion.

Double Romance from SIGNET

- [ ] **WHO IS LUCINDA?** by Hermina Black and **BITTER HONEY** by Hermina Black. (#E7630—$1.75)

- [ ] **LOST ISOBEL** by Katharine Newlin Burt and **REE** by Katharine Newlin Burt. (#W7506—$1.50)

- [ ] **SHEILA'S DILEMMA** by Ivy Valdes and **THE INTRUSION** by Elizabeth McCrae. (#W7440—$1.50)

- [ ] **THE ROOTS OF LOVE** by Vivian Donald and **LOVE FINDS THE WAY** by I. Torr. (#W7297—$1.50)

- [ ] **A CONFLICT OF WOMEN** by Emma Darby and **HAVEN OF PEACE** by I. Torr. (#W7370—$1.50)

- [ ] **THE ALIEN HEART** by Alice Lent Covert and **MAKE WAY FOR SPRING** by Peggy O'More. (#W7191—$1.50)

- [ ] **RETURN TO LOVE** by Peggy Gaddis and **ENCHANTED SPRING** by Peggy Gaddis. (#W7158—$1.50)

- [ ] **SECRET HONEYMOON** by Peggy Gaddis and **A HANDFUL OF MIRACLES** by Marion Naismith. (#Y6761—$1.25)

- [ ] **LOVING YOU ALWAYS** by Peggy Gaddis and **THE GIRL NEXT DOOR** by Peggy Gaddis. (#Y6760—$1.25)

- [ ] **EPISODE IN ROME** by Teri Lester and **SYLVIA'S DAUGHTER** by Ivy Valdes. (#W7264—$1.50)

THE NEW AMERICAN LIBRARY, INC.,
P.O. Box 999, Bergenfield, New Jersey 07621

Please send me the SIGNET BOOKS I have checked above. I am enclosing $_____(check or money order—no currency or C.O.D.'s). Please include the list price plus 35¢ a copy to cover handling and mailing costs. (Prices and numbers are subject to change without notice.)

Name_____

Address_____

City_____State_____Zip Code_____
Allow at least 4 weeks for delivery